PHILLIP

7 BRIDES FOR 7 BLACKTHORNES, BOOK #4

New York Times Bestselling Author

CRISTIN HARBER

ISBN: 978-1-951085-06-3

PROLOGUE

Twelve Years Ago
Harvard College

ASHLEY CARTWRIGHT STOOD in the center of the business school auditorium stage and fumbled over the well-practiced lines. For weeks, she'd prepared for the mock presentation to the shareholders and the board. But now, instead of the memorized lines that detailed the success of the mock business she'd worked on all semester, she only replayed the polite applause from her class after Dean Dunbar had introduced their special guest.

Famed lifestyle guru and media mogul Agatha Cartwright handled the limelight as though she were born for the attention, and with an air of perfection, she'd gracefully taken her seat next to the dean. Her mother had shown no sign of recognition when Ashley was randomly called as the first student to present.

Turning to glance at the presentation projected on the screen behind her, Ashley regathered her thoughts. "Several factors contributed to the company's growth." Sweat dampened the back of her neck, under her hair. She'd simply blown it out this morning. If she'd known she would come face-to-face with her mother, she would've worked to add volume and a hint of shine, something to draw attention from her unlined lips. They'd talked this morning! Not about anything great—mostly about the mistakes Ashley was making in her life—but her mother could've warned her. "Including a focus on pricing and cost control."

Her mother pinched her lips and jotted on her notepad. *What did I do wrong now?* She wondered if her mother had taken notes like that earlier when they were on the phone.

Ashley hated public speaking. She loved working behind the scenes. Ensuring that her mock company was a well-oiled machine had been fulfilling, but explaining the process was simply hell.

"Including p-pricing and cost control..." she stammered. Murmurs and whispers mixed with poorly disguised laughter. Humiliation crawled up her back. "I mean, with production volume rising quickly..."

Her mother continued writing feverishly.

A strange sound mixed with the students' laughter. She heard something like a *"baaa"* like an animal. *Ignore everyone. Don't watch Mother.* Ashley clenched her clammy hands, checked the presentation over her shoulder, and continued. "Meeting consumer demands."

"Baaaa."

The bleeting *"baaa"* called again as her peers quieted. Then the whispers began again. The next few seconds in her presentation were vital. The explanation of her company's success was the largest part of her grade. Failing in this very specific moment would've been the equivalent of a comic ruining his punch line.

She straightened her shoulders and lifted her chin, catching sight of her boyfriend at the top of the auditorium. Her heart squeezed. He'd promised he would be there, ready to make her laugh and relax during her speech. She rebounded at his encouraging smile, able to ignore the niggling concern that her mother would notice her fingernails weren't manicured.

"As demand grew, word of mouth grew." Her confidence grew. She clicked the button for the next slide. "The first peak on the chart marks organic growth. The second..." She accidentally glanced at the first row. Disapproval shadowed

Mother's gaze. "The second—"

"*Baaa. Baaa.*"

Another wave of murmuring laughter cascaded down the auditorium.

"Shhh! Easy!" A man's quiet commands mixed with the growing laughter.

Some students turned in their seats while others pointed toward the noises.

Dean Dunbar apologized to her mother and then turned from his front-row seat. "Quiet down."

"Stop. Stay," ordered the unseen man. "*Stay.*"

Concern skipped across Ashley's skin. That sounded like Phillip issuing dog commands. She scanned the room but couldn't see him anymore.

Gasps and giggles mixed with the bleating sound. An animal—a goat—clip-clopped quickly down the stairs, seemly unfazed. Phillip raced behind the goat, his arms open as though he were going to catch it. Ashley blinked, unable to make sense of the disaster but sick to her stomach that her boyfriend was behind it.

Her mother stood, and Ashley saw the exact moment of recognition. Disgust and disapproval creased the woman's forehead. Ashley glanced from her mother to her boyfriend and back again until he and the goat were in the center of the auditorium.

"What are you doing?" Ashley hoarsely cried.

Phillip stopped and gave an apologetic shrug. "I brought you a sensitivity goat."

Her jaw fell. She wasn't sure if her shock or anger was stronger. "You didn't..."

"Mr. Blackthorne," Dean Dunbar called out. "Is that your *goat?*"

"*Baaa. Baaa.*" The goat turned to face the auditorium. Several students stood to help Phillip. The goat spun and ran, skirting back and forth along the raised stage. Then it stopped at the stairs that led onto the stage and lifted a hoof to the first step.

"Don't," Ashley whispered.

"Billi," Phillip warned as he inched closer. "Stay."

The goat eyed him and perched its other hoof onto the first stair. Uproarious laughter broke out again. Two guys from the front row accompanied Phillip as they moved in.

Phillip offered her a conciliatory grin. "Surprise."

This time he'd gone too far with his tricks and fun. She would kill him—and oh, this was exactly what Mother had said was wrong with him. *Dangerously unpredictable and unstable.*

"Catch it," Dean Dunbar ordered.

Phillip and his wingmen approached, their arms spread. The goat bleated and clattered up the stairs. Raucous amusement filled the auditorium. Ashley jerked back as the goat skittered to center stage.

"You're on your own," one of the guys told Phillip.

"Sorry," the other said to her then lifted his shoulders in defeat. Both went back to their seats.

Phillip climbed on stage, cooing to the goat like he might coax it onto the leash and collar that hung from his hand.

The goat turned to Ashley, sniffing, and stepped closer. Its bright eyes wouldn't blink, and its wriggling nose seemed wet.

"Phillip," she hissed. "Catch it."

"Don't move." He closed in behind the goat. "Stay perfectly still."

The goat moved closer. Maybe it liked the flowers on her dress. "It's going to bite me."

"He won't." He inched closer. "Right, Billi? Billi Vanilli's a petting zoo goat. He's friendly. I promise he won't bite."

Billi Vanilli? Her hands trembled as the animal with a distinctive barnyard scent nuzzled her skirt. Its warm, snotty breath dampened the fabric against her knee. "It's touching me."

Phillip inched closer. "Don't move."

"Why do you have a goat?" she whispered, her voice shaking.

Phillip paused like she'd missed the obvious reason. "I promised you I'd come up with a distraction."

"What?"

"To help you relax during the big speech."

"Are you insane?" she hissed.

The goat jerked away as Phillip raised the collar near its neck.

"More like creative, but the little dude got loose," he suggested, reangling. *"Don't move.* I've almost got him."

Who on earth gave him a goat?

The goat spun to face Phillip head-on. Its hooves clattered as it backed toward her. Its backside pushed against her legs, barely missing her feet! Ashley jolted.

"Ash, don't move." Phillip held the leash out in a loop so he could wrap it around the goat's neck.

"Baaa." Billi shuffled in place. Its animal sounds echoed from the stage throughout the auditorium. Ashley made the mistake of turning toward her mother. She'd always hated Phillip, complaining about his lack of maturity. Ashley had never disagreed over that point with Mother. He wasn't the most responsible person she could have dated, and more than that, she would do anything for her mother to give her an ounce of approval.

Right now, that approval would never come. Mother's reaction had turned to cold indifference. The chasm between them felt like a public disowning.

Another sound came from the goat along with a sickening smell. "Ew! Oh God."

Phillip collared the goat. "Got you."

Plop. Plop. Plop.

"Phillip!" she cried, gagging. "No!"

He clipped the leash on as his eyes widened. "Oh, shit."

Laughter boomed through the auditorium. She staggered from the mess on the stage floor. His lips quirked, and he offered a helpless shrug.

Disgusted, stunned tears streamed down her face. Dean Dunbar called for a janitor and yelled for silence as her mother, Harvard's esteemed special guest, left without so much as a concerned glance or wave.

"That's..." Phillip couldn't finish without a laugh.

She wiped her cheeks, now the laughingstock of Harvard's campus.

"That's unfortunate," Phillip finally finished.

"Do you think this is funny?"

"Come on, Ash. It *is* funny."

"You think everything is funny! And if it isn't, you make it that way."

"Ease up." He gave her a sideways glance and tugged on the goat's leash as Dean Dunbar yelled for him to leave.

"Ease up?" she shouted, catching an awful whiff of the animal waste. "I can't do this anymore." She gagged, slapping her hands over her mouth.

Ashley stepped away and saw that the toes of her shoes had been *contaminated*. Her stomach turned. This time he'd gone too far. She kicked off her high heels as the goat bleated. The auditorium roared with laughter. The chaos surrounded her, strangling her, stealing her manners and compassion. "I hate you," she hissed.

Phillip, trying to lure the goat down the stage stairs, gave her another sideways glance.

He doesn't get it. "I'm done. I can't do this with you anymore." She turned away and ran.

CHAPTER ONE

Present Day
Upstate New York

*A*LL ALONE. WELL, Ashley wasn't really all alone, but that was how Agatha Cartwright would see Ashley's breakup from Sean Paget, the man her mother had set her up with. There had been an unagreed upon expectation that he would be *the one*. He wasn't even close.

Ashley smoothed her hands over the silk skirt recently highlighted in *Home* magazine. She'd worn it especially for her mother to note. Though, if she had, Mother hadn't mentioned it, despite the skirt having been front and center in this month's list of Mother's favorite things.

Ashley crossed her legs under the mahogany table, waiting in the formal dining room of her childhood home for Mother's lecture. It had taken several hours for Ashley to drive south to Upstate New York, but there she was, coming when called. All the therapy in the world hadn't helped her with that yet.

"The tulips are lovely," Ashley offered to kick off the conversation. That was true. The flowers were breathtaking. The entire home was always immaculate.

No matter if there were film crews on location to tape B-roll for Mother's nationally syndicated lifestyle show, or if it were a *simple* family dinner, the Cartwright residence sparkled. *Always picture perfect.*

"They are," Mother said in a way that confirmed rather

than agreed.

Ashley forced a grin but dropped her gaze to the square glass vases. Each had a ribbon tied near its top. Garden-fresh tulips packed each vase and lined the antique linen table runner in a way that softened the harsh dark wood.

But the antique table linen didn't soften her mother. With sharp features and perfect posture, Mother walked behind the chairs on the opposite side of the table. Her manicured fingernails trailed over the tops of the ornate high-back chairs.

"Mother?"

The older woman stilled then and turned, letting disapproval tug the corners of her coral-pink lips down.

Ashley refused to shrivel under the scorn. Even if she couldn't keep from coming home when called, she had mastered the ability to ignore the criticism… sort of. "Look, Mother—"

Her mother held up a hand. "Really, Ashley Catherine."

"I—"

"It's bad enough that you ended a fantastic relationship without cause—"

"Mother—"

The upheld hand shook for Ashley's silence. "But that I had to hear the news from Robert Paget is embarrassing."

True to form, Mother's concern was the family image, not how her daughter might feel. Ashley knew better, but still, disappointment roiled in her stomach. She also knew better than to say, "It's my life." Instead, Ashley offered, "We weren't a good fit."

Her mother's lips puckered. "That's not an excuse."

It wasn't supposed to be an excuse. It was a simple fact. She and Sean Paget were not the least bit compatible, not in love, not in life, not even in general. She couldn't see how Mother thought they were a good fit in any way except for the Paget surname. Still, the ever-present disappointment niggled at the back of her head. Even though Ashley was committed to living her own life and refused to kowtow to her mother's expectations, the sense of failure was never very far.

Ashley focused on the rhythm of her breath and regained control of her emotions. "That's what people do. They date, and if it's not right, they move on."

Her mother folded her arms over her cream-colored blouse. "The Paget family are not *people*."

"Actually, they are. I checked. Sean was human."

"You know exactly what I meant," Mother snapped.

Her shoulders slumped. "Yeah, Mother, I do."

As though the conversation made Mother weary, she pinched the bridge of her nose. "I don't know what I'm going to do with you."

"You could do *nothing*." But that suggestion never helped. Ashley could be straightforward, shouting that she was her daughter, not a business in the market for an acquisition. Or she could mention a hope for romantic love.

Her mother clucked. "If I'd known you'd become harder to manage the older you got—"

Ashley called upon years spent with a therapist to stand up to her mother's iron will. "Please, stop. My love life isn't a topic for conversation." Even though she knew it was the topic du jour when her mother demanded an appearance.

The sleeves and neck of her shirt seemed to cinch tighter. She rested her palm over her stomach and carefully monitored each slow breath, reminding herself that she was in charge of her response. Then Ashley offered a different approach. "I'm sorry you were put in an embarrassing position." She swallowed her aggravation. "I never meant to upset you."

Mother's chin lifted as she placed both hands on the top of the chair. A small grin formed in place of the scowl. "I appreciate that."

But silence lingered. Ashley hadn't said enough.

She searched for what else her mother wanted to hear,

then offered, "The relationship ended amicably."

That comment got no reaction.

"And… and we intend to remain in close contact." *Still nothing.* "As friends."

"Ashley Catherine…" Her mother eased into the chair. "I'm looking out for you."

"I promise I'm fine."

"You have no companion. No one in your corner."

Ashley bit her tongue. Mother didn't see that as the job of a family. Her father was happily aloof in his own world, which revolved around Wall Street. Her mother's life revolved around making everything perfect. Together, Glenn and Agatha Cartwright made a terrific power couple, happy together as it served their individual and professional needs.

"I have my friends," Ashley pointed out. "My company."

Pity creased the corners of her mother's mouth. "I can't see how you have provided for yourself."

The truth was, she was lucky. Still, Ashley's molars sawed together. Yes, she came from a well-off family, she'd inherited an amazing place to live, and she'd had the privilege of a Harvard education to top off family business lessons. But in addition to that, she was tenacious, even if a bit stubborn. That had given her the gumption to provide for herself, even if she hadn't pursued the corporate executive lifestyle her mother had assumed she would take within Cartwright Media, the conglomerate corporation that owned the corresponding companies for the magazine, television show, home goods, and whatever else existed.

Picture Perfect, her event company, was all of her own making, and Ashley enjoyed the behind-the-scenes action. "I provide for myself, and it's fulfilling."

Mother mouthed, "fulfilling," her feathers seemingly ruffled. "The Paget family offers stability, reliability, an impeccable image that would only enhance your little"—she waved her hand—"company."

Ashley rebuffed the condescension and focused on her breathing. "That's all fine and good, but I want to fall in love."

"Like I said, you used to listen and ignore such foolishness."

The jab hit like a spear through her heart. "Ignoring the foolishness" had served as a pivotal point in her life. Ashley might've walked away from love, but she pictured how her life might be if she'd continued in Agatha Cartwright's *perfect* steps. Perfectly corporate and perfectly miserable.

The jab at Ashley's foolishness had been what Mother considered a dismissal. Without a goodbye, she left the immaculate table, and Ashley was, thankfully, alone again—except for the turmoil consuming her thoughts: Phillip Blackthorne. He was the most irresponsible and worst decision of her life, hands down. Falling in love with him. Running away from him. Phillip had been a lesson she'd had to learn on her own, even if the rise and fall of their love still seared her heart.

CHAPTER TWO

King Harbor, Maine

PHILLIP BLACKTHORNE LEANED into the corner of his golf cart as it edged the immaculate path up the hills that made King Harbor Country Club's golf course legendary. Someone needed to note the balance of their golf carts, too, Phillip mused. The award-winning course was one thing. But a golf cart that he couldn't bring onto just two wheels? That was a completely different challenge that he was ready to accept.

The cart skated into the manicured greens, still on four wheels. Phillip roared with laughter. His brother Brock, not so much.

But Phillip had had to do something to ward off the anxious knot building in his chest when Brock broached the topic of Aunt Claire walking out on Uncle Graham at her sixtieth birthday party. Brock worried over the potential for corporate fallout and how outsiders would see the Blackthorne brand.

Phillip had no such worries and avoided family problems with distractions and adrenaline shots while his youngest brother, Brock, ate stress for breakfast, so long as it was properly branded with the barrel and thistle logo.

They bounced from the trail to the green and back onto the path again. Brock might not approve, but Phillip would bet his Callaways that his brother was having a hell of a good time.

"Enough," Brock barked, seemingly unruffled.

They bounced hard over a bump, and Phillip cut a sharp turn. "What?" He gassed the cart on a straightaway. "I couldn't hear you." They rumbled over a dip, and their drinks sloshed from their sweating plastic cups.

"If someone sees you acting like a jackass," Brock said, "who do you think will clean up that mess?"

"Relax. We're home free." Phillip jabbed his elbow toward his youngest brother. "No one comes over here."

They reached the top of a hill at full speed, and his stomach lurched as they crested, hitting a small swell hard. The cart jumbled back and forth before making a downhill streak. Phillip worked the steering wheel, but it seemed too loose.

"Phillip," Brock shouted. "Watch out."

He glanced down the long hill. A large event tent covered the open space between the thick barrier of trees on either side. "Shit!"

Phillip hit the brakes. A mechanical whir whined from below his feet. His foot pressed the brake pedal to the floor. Nothing happened. He pumped the pedal again, and still nothing happened. Adrenaline rocketed into his blood.

"The brakes?" Brock demanded.

He shook his head. "They're gone." Phillip jiggled the steering wheel. Their trajectory remained unchanged. "And the steering's gone too."

"You've got to be joking." Brock glanced from the tent to the steering column. "Turn it off. Turn the key."

He was already trying that. "It won't budge." They were running out of time, and he didn't want to die today.

"We can't hit that," Brock said, stating the obvious. "Not if people are in there."

"And 'cause we don't want to die," Phillip muttered, pressing the brake pedal to the floor and trying in vain to change course. They had less than a minute to figure out what to do. "We have to bail out."

"Are you insane?" Brock threw his arm toward the tent.

"We jump out and do our best to knock the cart over."

Brock's jaw ticked.

"Or at least off course." Phillip jerked the steering wheel and attacked the brakes. "Have a better plan?"

"I told you to act like a Blackthorne." Brock tried to rock the cart. "You never learn."

Phillip ignored Brock and kneeled on his seat. "Out the back. If we jump together, it might turn."

Brock shook his head as they both climbed over their seats, precariously balancing next to their golf clubs.

Phillip looked over his shoulder at the tent. "Ready?"

Brock grumbled.

It was now or never. "One, two, three!"

★ ★ ★

THE MAGICAL SOUND of happy guests chattering over leafy greens and the finest white wine filled both the tent and Ashley's heart. The Laumet Society's charity luncheon was, thus far, the pinnacle of her event-planning career. Even though she was grandfathered, or rather, grandmothered, into the exclusive club, her membership was only considered social, which didn't mean much. She'd had to schmooze her way into handling this event, beating out well-known party and event planners. But she'd done it! The luncheon she'd spent nearly a year planning was now underway as the string quartet transitioned to "Amazing Grace."

Lori Wynell, the local-news television reporter, smoothed her hair behind her ear. "We're one minute out."

Ashley swallowed over the knot in her throat. "Great." While planning the charity event couldn't have gone any better, she would do nearly anything to avoid live television. Public speaking was her Achilles' heel. But Bitsy Montauk, reigning Laumet Society president for at least a decade, left her no choice, pushing her toward the camera with only polite introductions and strict instructions to share The Laumet Society's charity app.

Ashley could do that. How hard could it be to answer a few questions and explain how to participate in the online silent auction? Perhaps the camera would spend more time on the array of donation items than her.

Either way, after a lifetime of instruction from her mother on graceful presentation, she could do this. Ashley balanced her weight in such a way that she kept her slingback heels from sinking into the thick carpet of perennial ryegrass. The golf course at the King Harbor Country Club looked like an emerald velvet rug. The cool, thin blades were perfect for golfing. But high heels, not so much.

"Ready?" Lori asked Ashley as her camerawoman, Trinity, moved into place.

You can do this. She nodded and focused on the delicate clink of silverware against china plates that filtered through the high-vaulted ceiling of the air-conditioned tent. "Yes."

In the background, tuxedoed waitstaff worked their way through the elegant tables, clearing the salads and serving Maine lobster panzanella. She could picture each dish, garnished with grilled corn and roasted tomatoes, as clearly as she could recall each salad plate, with the decorative drizzles of olive oil and sprinkles of lemon zest. Everything was simply perfect.

Trinity extended five fingers. Lori cleared her throat, spoke to the newsroom, then to Ashley. "This will be a piece of cake."

She hoped so. "Let's get it over with."

Lori smiled as though she understood Ashley's nerves. Trinity signaled two seconds out, one, and showtime.

"Thanks, and that's right, we are at the King Harbor Country Club, where The Laumet Society is hosting their annual luncheon and silent auction."

Ashley's heart skipped as Lori focused on her.

"Ashley Catherine Cartwright, the leading lady behind Picture Perfect, is here to share details about how viewers at home can participate in the charity auction."

She leaned toward Lori's microphone and wondered where to look. *At Lori or the camera?* She decided to do some of both. "The Laumet Society raises funds to help Maine's homeless families, particularly their children, have a safe place to go, especially when the weather turns cold."

Trinity glanced from her camera as Ashley paused, thinking that Lori would jump in for another question. The reporter paused briefly, unsaid questions passing between her and Trinity, before she asked, "How can viewers at home participate?"

Ashley recalled Bitsy's wording. "This is the first year we've taken bids online. Anyone at home—"

"Move!" Trinity waved her arm. "Move! Now!"

Shocked, Ashley and Lori faltered, their high heels catching in the grass. Trinity pushed them aside, and they fell as a golf cart crashed into their tent.

CHAPTER THREE

T HE GOLF CART tore through the canvas tent wall and crashed into the silent auction table. Ashley gasped as the table turned. The string quartet screeched to a stop. Guests yelled and fled as silverware and plates crashed.

Everyone ran for safety except Ashley, Lori, and Trinity. The newscast duo morphed from society duty into recounting a catastrophe, narrating the collapse of the far side tent wall.

Ashley pulled herself up and gaped at the damage. "Is anyone hurt?"

"Anyone hurt?" immediately echoed, but in deep baritone voices. "Is everyone okay?"

She turned toward the voices. Two men rushed into the damaged tent and stopped, surveying the destruction.

Shell-shocked, Ashley did again as well. They were lucky no one had been in the direct line of the golf cart that now was pinned between two tables.

The scent of burning rubber hung in the air. Sirens rang in the distance. People could have died! Her legs wobbled as an ice sculpture crashed. She and Lori yelped as Trinity swung her camera toward the men.

Their dark hair was ruffled, and their crisp polo shirts grass stained. Her gaze narrowed, and another rush of anxiety hit. "Brock?"

He stopped, blocking the identity of the other man behind him, but Ashley would know him anywhere, even when masked by the unusual longer hair and stubble. Brock's focus on the camera registered the seriousness of the situation, and she could've sworn he mouthed a silent curse. But that was Brock, ready for the camera, always confident and controlled.

And if that was Brock, and this was a disaster... Her stomach turned. *Years of avoidance.* For years, she'd changed her plans and done everything to avoid her ex since the day she'd broken their hearts and run away.

Phillip stepped into her clear view.

"Oh God." Her hand clutched her chest at the sight of Phillip Blackthorne—the king of shenanigans and skirter of responsibility, the only man she'd ever loved. He was a paradox of playfulness and deep, hidden emotions. A flood of embarrassment and anxiety nearly took her to the ground.

Brock strode forward, greeting all in his professional tone.

Phillip came alongside his brother, greeting only her. "Ashley."

Her name on his lips made her weak. She needed to hold on to the disaster that surrounded them, remember that this was who he was, and what happened when he was around. But her heart nearly screamed.

"Phillip." Tears burned her throat. "Hello." She didn't know why she ached or how to make that pain go away.

"It's been a while." His jawline had sharpened over the years, but his dark, playful eyes remained the same, dancing and daring her to hide anything from him.

But something in him had changed beyond surface level. She didn't know what and shouldn't care. Their differences needed to keep her from him.

"It has," she admitted. Heat rose to her cheeks as did a tornado of emotions. She had been angry and a coward when she'd run off the stage at Harvard. She'd also been weak and far too easy to influence. All the years she'd thought about apologizing to him, wondering about the possibility of what they could have been, but knowing, despite her immature means, the breakup had been the right decision.

Ashley swallowed but then came back to the here and now. She was surrounded by everything she needed to know about Phillip's irresponsibility. But this time, his recklessness had nearly killed her. Just like her mother had said, Phillip was a risky disaster. And her mother, famously, was never wrong.

Brock abruptly turned toward the reporter and camerawoman, reminding Ashley they were still there. As if the acknowledgment gave Lori permission, she launched at Brock with a tirade of questions. Always unfazed, he shifted the conversation and the reporter's line of sight away from her and Phillip and the damage to an unmarred tent wall with large plastic picture windows that overlooked the green.

Phillip cocked his head, stepping to Ashley's side. "Small world."

"Small world," she managed, tight-jawed.

The corners of his lips quirked. "You don't look happy to see me."

Oh, the jokes. His irresponsible quips came roaring back. "That might be the understatement of the summer." Her teeth tapped, a mixture of nervous energy and sudden irritation—both at him and herself. "I'm not thrilled to see you."

"Consider me shocked." He smirked. "Would you like to scurry off? I think Brock has this handled, and you're so good at running away."

Her molars ground together. "This is the wrong time to turn us around on me."

"There is no us. Remember?" He crossed his arms. "You decided that years ago."

"A lot of good that did me." She was a strong woman. Perhaps stubborn, somewhat too strong for her own good, but she likened her resolve to steel in so many situations. *Unmoving. Unyielding.* Steel was the strongest metal known to man, impact resistant and unscathed when pulled in opposite directions. Right now, that was what she needed to be.

Phillip dabbed at a cut above his eyebrow, masking a small wince.

"Are you—" She made herself stop. He had a small cut when he could've killed people. That was what she needed to focus on.

"Ashley," Lori called, snaring her attention.

The camera swung toward her and Phillip, and worry creased Brock's forehead. But she was a professional—even if petrified of public speaking—and he knew she would handle herself under pressure. They'd worked together, fixing problems behind the scenes before, though nothing of this magnitude. Ashley straightened her shoulders and stepped toward the camera, reminding herself to be steel, and listened for what Lori would ask next.

"There she goes, leaving again," Phillip muttered under his breath.

Brock seemed to sense the brooding trouble and loudly, if not smoothly, pulled the camera's attention back toward him.

That was her cue to get rid of Phillip. With an elegant turn, she whispered, "Go away."

"Not yet."

Ashley wanted to shake that smug, cocky half grin from his face. Instead, her hands clenched, and she muttered, "To think, I forgot how I hated you."

Phillip cackled as though that were what he was hoping to hear. "Glad to see nothing has changed."

Gah! She hated this… *feeling*, whatever it was.

Lori cleared her throat.

Ashley focused on the waiting microphone. Embarrassment rocketed up her spine, flushing heat across her face. Her stomach turned as Lori repeated her question, and Brock, again out of the frame, mouthed, "We're still live."

CHAPTER FOUR

THIS WAS THE second time that day Phillip had felt like he was having an out-of-body experience. The first had been when he and Brock had rolled from the golf cart—and lived— only to run toward the event tent, terrified that he'd killed people inside.

The second was occurring now. Brock and Ashley morphed into caricatures of themselves, impeccable on-air talent. Caricature or not, Ashley was riveting with her effortless laughter and easygoing banter. Phillip wanted her to act more like Agatha Cartwright—uptight and a pain in the ass. That would make Ashley easier to dislike. Hell, that had been what he'd held on to when they broke up, telling himself he'd dodged a bullet.

And what a gorgeous bullet he'd dodged. Phillip eased back, continuing to watch her. Ashley gracefully laughed off their personal spectacle, and Brock made a joke about how Blackthornes lived under a microscope.

Even as they talked, Ashley's words ran through his head. *I hate you.* He couldn't stop the replay, just like he couldn't forget the punch in the gut when he'd first seen her today, scared, worried, then angry when she saw who she could blame.

I hate you. He wanted to hate her, too. She'd had his heart then torched it, even though he might have deserved it.

Phillip needed to walk away, but he couldn't move. Even though he'd heard she lived in King Harbor, he'd avoided her at every opportunity. But now, an arm's length away, he was her captive.

The reporter inched closer to Brock. Phillip could tell she'd readied a hard-nosed question, and he almost grinned. It would take more than knocking down a charity tent and airing an old romance grievance for Brock to falter.

"The damage appears to be extensive," the reporter said.

Phillip noted how Ashley's jaw tightened. The tip of her tongue darted out, wetting her bottom lip, as she tried to relax. No one would notice. It was an old habit that he remembered. A trip down memory lane came, and he recalled far more about those lips, that tongue... The back of his neck warmed, and he shifted, rubbing a hand into his hair.

"The golf cart collided with a hundred thousand dollars of donations." The reporter dangled each word like she hoped for a Daytime Emmy. "*Maybe* even more."

Brock took the question with convincing charisma, effortlessly answering as if it had been scripted and planned.

The theatrics aggravated Phillip, and he shoved his hands into his pockets. But he also became increasingly uncomfortable, and he glanced at the upturned table. A hundred thousand dollars of donations? If it has been his nonprofit Project Sunshine, they would've taken a massive hit if donations he expected to help fund his summer camp didn't come.

Phillip ballparked the cost to pull off an event of such magnitude. The budget alone had to be five figures. Golf course rental, catering, music, tables with flowers that he knew Ashley had planned to match her clothes. Or maybe it had been the other way around, and the flowers had come first. Either way, he'd screwed over a nonprofit. That was a world he knew better than Brock, maybe better than Ashley.

"Was this an accident or incident?" the reporter asked in a way that pulled Phillip back to the interview.

Brock grinned. "Is this one of those questions where we

debate what the definition of *is* is?"

Ashley and the reporter laughed. Phillip didn't. It wasn't *that* funny.

Brock's explanation only strayed slightly from the truth, but the reporter tried again. They volleyed *how and why* in their fruitless tete-a-tete. It wasn't as if Brock would simply explain that Phillip had careened a golf cart down a hill like a thoroughbred leading at the Derby.

Their voices mixed with King Harbor's summer air, which lifted Ashley's hair as it rolled through the damaged tent. A dull, needy ache squeezed his chest. She was beautiful in a way that had always torn the breath from his lungs.

At Harvard, Brock had told Phillip he didn't have a chance. Phillip couldn't remember how long it had taken to convince his younger brother to introduce him to Brock's freshman dorm resident adviser. But after Brock gave in, the rest was history—including the part where Brock had promised they would never last.

They hadn't. Brock had been right. That hadn't stopped Phillip from falling in love.

Brock gestured to Ashley, his hand glancing off her elbow. A sudden irritation crawled across Phillip as though ants swarmed under his skin. He studied their interactions, the friendly way the conversation flowed. Nothing inappropriate occurred. They were consummate professionals. Yet there was an unmistakable friendly familiarity.

Phillip inched closer and searched his memory, unable to recall Brock mentioning Ashley. If they'd stayed in touch beyond Harvard, no one had told him. Phillip crossed his arms and stepped closer as a resentful heaviness settled in his gut.

Again, Brock gestured to Ashley. "Our family will make this right, and I'll ensure Ms. Cartwright has whatever resources are needed."

The friendly touches. The flawless banter. A tightness

bubbled in his chest. The temperature inside the damaged tent rose another hundred degrees, and his polo shirt cinched like a straitjacket. "I'll do it." Phillip joined the on-air conversation before his mind understood what the hell his mouth had done.

Ashley's mouth fell open, but she recovered. Brock's expression was unreadable.

The reporter and camerawoman adjusted to fit Phillip in their frame. Phillip didn't care what Brock would say, and he faced Ashley. "We will work this out."

He wasn't sure what he'd meant by his offer, but by God, Phillip was the Blackthorne that Ashley would spend time with if there was work to be done with their family.

Her eyes questioned his sanity, and her thinned lips yelled for him to go away, but to the rest of the world, she remained unemotional and composed, a talent she likely could thank her mother for.

"We'll work *together*." Brock clapped a hand on Phillip's back. The visual seemed brotherly, but the message between brothers was crystal clear. *Stand down.* "Our family works together as a team, and we'll do more than raise money. We'll raise awareness. It's time for Maine to have an honest conversation about the resources dedicated to—"

"Consider me leading the conversation." In that unscripted moment, Phillip understood he was a jealous man. "You can work with me."

Brock cleared his throat. "Exactly. As a team."

Phillip didn't care how Brock cleaned up this mess. He had things to tell Ashley. "I fix my mistakes. It's a thing I've done well since you've been gone."

Her lips flattened, but an unmistakable flare burned in her eyes. "I never went anywhere."

"But you sure disappeared." He closed the distance between them, and their proximity hit him like a drug. "I screwed up, but this time, you'll see that I will fix it."

"Another screwup." Her voice cracked as she whispered, "Something new for a change."

Brock's nostrils flared, and his teeth clenched. "*Phillip.*"

"And that brings us to the most important question." The reporter thrust her microphone between Phillip and Ashley. "Will The Laumet Society meet their fund-raising goal?"

Ashley swung toward the reporter. "Absolutely."

"Would it be possible without the assistance from the Blackthornes?"

Ashley gulped.

"They can when they partner with Project Sunshine," Phillip interrupted, throwing his nonprofit into the mix. "Our annual charity car show is two weeks away. Together, we'll surpass whatever The Laumet Society intended to raise today."

Ashley's lips parted. Brock's jaw ticked, the only sign of his annoyance at being unable to wrangle the spiraling situation. The reporter's eyes glittered at the soap-opera-like show. But Phillip wouldn't walk away until he got what he wanted—Ashley's agreement.

"It would work if…" Her wheels were turning, calculating the hope and aggravation that would be required to work together and reach an enormous goal. "Both charities could meet their goals if you donated your 330 GT."

His *Ferrari 330 GT*?

She might've said *your baby*. Her request landed like a sucker punch. Damn, Phillip loved to hate that car. If she knew its history, Ashley wouldn't have asked. She might hate him, but she wasn't cruel. Its value clocked in at nearly five hundred thousand dollars, but its worth was priceless.

His heart hammered. Losing the car but spending time with her? A deep breath pained his chest as he agreed. "Deal. I'll auction off my Ferrari."

CHAPTER FIVE

Trinity finished packing her camera bag as Lori made her way to Ashley feverishly working on her phone from an untouched table. There wasn't anything on her phone that commanded her full attention, including her mother's incessant phone calls, but Ashley wasn't ready to continue the conversation with Brock and Phillip.

Lori pulled up a chair. "If this doesn't pull the highest ratings we've ever had, then I don't know what more Mainers want."

Ashley wished that weren't true. She laid her phone on the table as Trinity waved goodbye, lugging her equipment toward a golf cart they'd used to transport their gear from the parking lot.

The reporter produced her business card and gave Ashley's forearm a friendly squeeze. "I'll reach out to you for a follow-up."

"That's fine." Of course they would want a follow-up. They'd just given Mainers a soap opera, live on air, complete with billionaires and romantic tension. "Next time will be a lot calmer."

"For my sake, I hope not." Lori laughed, then added, "But for yours, I'll cross my fingers."

Ashley held up crossed fingers then waved goodbye. Once Lori and Trinity were a safe distance away, she discreetly glanced at Brock and Phillip. They stood outside the tent, visible through one of the faux windows, surrounded by the who's who of The Laumet Society.

Finally alone, Ashley really took in what had happened. It was the first moment that she realized someone had hung yellow tape around the tent as if they were standing in the middle of a crime scene.

Her eyes sank shut. How very like King Harbor not to interrupt a television spot filled with high-society drama over the concern of a building's stability. But what did she know? Perhaps the swaying tent was safe. Someone would've had enough sense to let them know if they were in danger, live TV or not.

The gaggle of women noticed Ashley was alone and diverted the group into the tent. Chitchat filtered in, led by Bitsy. Catering staff with table bussing tubs entered from the far corner. The musicians made their way to their abandoned instruments. Ashley met Bitsy midway, greeting The Laumet ladies while avoiding a glance about to see if Phillip and Brock remained nearby.

"No one was hurt, and the press coverage will glow!" Bitsy cried, taking Ashley's hands in hers. "You were magnificent. We couldn't have paid for that type of television coverage."

She gaped. "You watched?"

"From the clubhouse. More than one station reported." She beckoned Phillip and Brock as they reentered the tent.

Her cheeks flushed. "Oh."

The Blackthorne brothers stood next to Bitsy, and she rested her hand on Phillip's arm. "This partnership is brilliant. We're so grateful—"

"It's the least I can do," he volunteered.

Their pleasant tones bordered on friendly. Grateful, even. Ashley stepped back, unsettled, and she gestured to the damage. "What about—"

"That's what insurance is for." Bitsy waved her concern away. "No one was hurt, and we monopolized the news."

"You've gone viral," another lady added, sounding as

though she'd just learned what the word meant.

Oh God. *Viral?* Her phone rang again, and Ashley's money was on Mother calling for the hundredth time. That kind of stress could be handled later.

"It's all over the internet," the woman added. "My granddaughter called to say we were famous."

"Great…"

Bitsy took Brock by the elbow and led him to the upturned silent auction table. The remaining Laumet ladies flanked them, pitching a request for a donation from Blackthorne Enterprises.

"They know when it's a good time to strike," Phillip pointed out.

They were finally alone. His very presence was palpable despite the space between them, intoxicating her with head-spinning desires to be closer.

Phillip eased forward, somehow able to read her mind or maybe craving more of their obvious connection. Her heart skipped, reminding her of the first time they'd found themselves alone at Harvard, when an electric charge skimmed down her back and promised he was the one. He'd been magnetic, and he still was.

That attraction could be dangerous. She shifted, ignoring her roller coaster of reactions, and struggled to make small talk. "Is the cut above your eye okay?" she asked.

His fingers touched the newly formed scab. "I'll live."

"Good to hear."

His crooked grin formed, and he subtly devoured the slight space between them. "I thought so."

A cascade of awareness swept across her skin. The delicious sensation made her unsteady. Desire bloomed deep, but it warred with logic. She swallowed hard. "Don't be so cavalier. You could've killed people."

"I'm not, and I know."

She glared, searching for the anger that she used to keep

her reaction to him at bay. It didn't come. Desperate to extinguish her rapidly heating emotions, she snapped, "Why are you doing this? Let Brock clean up your mess."

His eyes narrowed. "Why not? I screwed up. I'll fix it."

His flippancy was just what she needed, and Ashley rolled her eyes. "As if it's just that easy."

"It is," he countered.

"Ha." She snorted. "Maybe you should do the heavy lifting and learn what responsibility really takes."

He chuckled. "Nothing about you has ever been easy." His gaze dropped to her lips and lingered. "Guess we'll see what you can teach me."

She shivered. "Don't do that."

"Do what, Ashley?" His eyes roamed down her neck to her dress, and when she thought she might melt, they drifted back up to her face again. "I haven't done a thing. Except"— he extended his arms—"create a disaster... or a brilliant public relations move, depending on who you ask."

His cocky bravado cooled her scorching reaction to how he studied her, serving as a reminder of who he was. A man that couldn't be serious. Dangerously so. It'd been hard to walk away from him, but the future was now, and she knew breaking up had been the right decision.

"Nothing to say?" he quipped.

Ashley shifted, trying to keep her high heels from sinking into the grass, and ignored him. She waited for him to leave. The minutes crawled by, and Phillip didn't move an inch. The longer he kept quiet and stayed close, the heavier the urge to run became. She needed distance, needed her sanity. If he didn't leave, she might snap and had no idea what that would mean.

Her heartbeat ticked in her ears like the second hand of a clock she couldn't avoid. Every single beat yelled for her to escape. Ashley spun away. "I can't do this."

"Hang on."

Her quick departure was hamstrung by her high heels caught in the soft grass.

His hand clamped onto her right shoulder, and his fingers gently flexed. "Ashley, stop."

Her pulse pounded, and inexplicably, tears clogged her throat. She couldn't run, couldn't stay, and her useless legs refused to help her flee. Defeated, she twisted to face the man she desperately wanted to hate. "What?"

He licked his bottom lip then rolled his mouth together. His nostrils slowly flared as he pulled a deep inhale, letting it out just as slowly. "I'm sorry."

"Good," she managed.

"About this." He squeezed her arm before letting go. "And before."

Before... There was so much he didn't know about before.

Bitsy materialized next to their conversation. "I understand you two used to date."

Phillip's grin made Ashley so sad. "Used to."

"Used to," she needlessly added, hating to agree with the truth.

Bitsy glanced from Phillip to Ashley, eyes dancing as she studied their dynamic. "My, it's already been an exciting day. I wonder what the future will bring."

CHAPTER SIX

THE BLAZING AFTERNOON sun burned the back of Phillip's neck. Or maybe that was the stain of the hot streak Ashley had singed from his neck to his chest. His and Brock's golf clubs had been caddied to the Range Rover they'd borrowed from the Blackthorne estate, reaching the black SUV before them. They'd opted to walk. Both needed time to stretch their legs and let their minds roam.

Phillip knew as soon as they reached the safety of the Range Rover, Brock would break from the PR-perfect presence he'd maintained in public and ream his ass.

Phillip unlocked the vehicle, and they loaded their waiting bags and took their seats without a word. The tension grew in the tight space, making the hot air hard to breathe, but thankfully, the air-conditioning was as quick to cool.

Brock readjusted his glasses. "Do you think you can get us home without a problem?"

Phillip weighed his response. Usually, when he saw Brock wearing his glasses, Phillip took that as a sign his brother might relax—or at least try to. But he didn't know which Brock sat beside him. The one concerned about the family brand, or the one who couldn't think of his brother as anything other than a troublemaker. Phillip shifted the Range Rover into reverse. "Are you going to be a pain about this all day?"

Brock grumbled. "Yeah. I was thinking about it."

"You were there." His jaw clenched. "You know it was an

accident."

"You've said that your whole life."

Phillip's nostrils flared. Whether or not that had been a jab over their parents' death, he didn't know. But it wouldn't have been the first time Brock placed the blame for their deaths on his shoulders.

He straightened the car and shifted to drive. His fingers tightened around the smooth, polished steering wheel, and he let the dig go, more interested in what was still simmering under his skin. "What's up with you and Ashley?"

"Excuse me?" Brock's brow furrowed. "Meaning what, exactly?"

Phillip ground his teeth as he drove out of the parking lot. "You've stayed in contact."

"Is that a question or a statement?" Brock asked.

Jealousy stabbed at his back. "How about that?"

"Why wouldn't we?"

His nostrils flared. "I don't know. You're so into Team Blackthorne that it seems obvious to side with your flesh and blood and not my ex."

Brock chuckled. "I didn't take sides."

His fingers flexed tight on the steering wheel. "You never mentioned it."

"What are you? Twelve years old? She's a business acquaintance."

Phillip sawed his teeth. "Did you *see* her?"

"As in, did I date her?" Brock snorted, testing the last threads of Phillip's patience. "I don't date every beautiful woman I know."

Beautiful grated his nerves. Did he trust his brother? Yeah. Yet Brock hadn't explicitly said no. "Keep talking."

"You know I play my relationships close to the vest," Brock continued.

As they all did. There were times their last name attracted the wrong kind of attention just as there were times, like today, when their last name gave them some slack.

"But never at work, and never with her." Brock glanced over at him. "I've worked with Ashley before when she coordinated a few small events over the years for Blackthorne Enterprises. Maybe Devlin's worked with her on something for Boatworks. I don't know. She's good at what she does."

Ashley had a knack for business. Phillip wondered why she and Brock hadn't been the ones to date in college. He was more her type, with his eye for public perception and all-around predictability. Brock would have earned Agatha Cartwright's seal of approval, and he sure as hell wouldn't have let a goat crap on Ashley's shoe.

"Relax," Brock said. "Besides, if you hadn't wrecked her event, I would've said you two looked good together today."

Phillip laughed. "Right."

"You never know. Opposites attract." He laughed. "In college, I'd have bet money that you wouldn't have made it beyond a week."

That had been Phillip's fear once. Then everything had, more or less, worked out. He'd envisioned their lives together. Once, he'd even owned an engagement ring. Phillip snorted, driving in silence to the family compound with the past on his mind. With every passing coastal mile, Ashley held court over his thoughts, one memory coming to light after the next.

Finally, their home came into view. Home was an understatement, but that was what it had been to them during the summers. Their home in Boston had been equally as large and grand. Or rather, both of his homes in Boston had been—the one with his parents, and the one they'd moved into with his aunt and uncle and their kids when fall came around.

Moving in with Graham and Claire at the start of the school year had been one of the first moments it felt as though his parents were really gone. Aunt Claire had done everything she could to ease the transition from King Harbor to Boston. Much of his life had remained the same, including their school, friends, and schedules. But Phillip couldn't forget how it felt to settle into his new bedroom. It was as if that first night he'd finally grasped that his mom and dad were never coming back.

Phillip opted to park in the front drive and pulled the Range Rover behind Devlin's black Audi. Too many memories hammered Phillip, and he needed to escape, pushing out his door almost before he'd killed the ignition.

Brock wasn't far behind as Phillip pushed through the front door and through the formal entryway. He caught a glimpse of himself in an oversized antique mirror that lined the sprawling foyer, and he stopped short. The corners of his eyes were crinkled. His hair was better kept. He'd filled out and aged, looking every bit the thirty-three years he was. But for the last few hours, he'd felt younger, more foolish, and unable to control his surroundings. Thinking of his parents and Ashley had sent him into a tailspin of misery and heartache.

He turned from his reflection and headed into the living room. Hannah, her eyes wide with curiosity, and Devlin, with an eyebrow crooked, sat on the couch as though they'd been waiting. Bitsy's mention of viral publicity surfaced, and Phillip immediately deciphered their looks. "You saw?"

Hannah offered an exaggerated, "Yes."

"I didn't know if you'd kill each other or kiss," Devlin joked. "But, wow, the Ferrari?"

Killing, kissing, and cars. None were topics he wanted to discuss. "I have to get to work."

"You can't leave us hanging," Hannah said.

Brock ambled in from the kitchen, a whisky in hand. "This should be good."

Devlin eyed Brock. "Ashley handled that well, huh?"

Phillip glared. Despite the warning on Boatworks, the casual way they mentioned her name made his envy curl. "Everybody's chummy."

Brock laughed, cluing Devlin in. "He didn't realize we've worked with her."

Devlin shrugged. "She's great."

"Matter of opinion," Phillip muttered.

Hannah laughed. "Wow."

"To be honest," Brock added, "I've enjoyed watching her company grow."

Phillip waved his brother's admission away. Resentment built in his chest. "I've heard enough." Then he added under his breath, "*Traitors.*"

"I didn't keep it from you." Devlin chuckled and draped his arm behind Hannah. "You were in DC, and it was business as normal."

Brock eased onto the couch closest to the double-sided fireplace and sipped the whisky. "Given your reaction, I don't know if I would've told you anyways."

Phillip rubbed his hand over the back of his neck. They didn't know how he'd been hurt, only how stupid the goat incident had been. "Just because I wasn't her type didn't mean it wasn't real."

Hannah leaned into Devlin. Brock's amusement dampened. But Phillip didn't want their pity.

"Look, I never said you weren't her type." Brock's bemusement was now a sympathetic smile. "I simply said that it could never last."

CHAPTER SEVEN

A SHLEY WALKED INTO the beach house that she and her best friend, Mary Beth, called home. The familiar white shiplap walls always offered what felt like a hug after she pushed through the heavy wood door. She'd come to think of it as her grandmother welcoming her home.

Her home. She'd inherited the beach house and taken special steps to painstakingly modernize it while ensuring she didn't lose that connection to her grandmother. From the bright-white painted beams overhead to the coastal-blue accent pieces, Ashley had poured herself into her home like she had her company.

The only downside to her home was that Mother treated it as though she had an open invitation to show up at the *family* beach house.

Ashley corrected her until she'd given up. There was a reason her grandmother hadn't left the house to Mother, and Ashley mused that her mother had once been more like a person than a corporate machine. But after that persona had taken hold, she couldn't appreciate the family beach house anymore. That was why it had simply become Ashley's treasured home.

She crossed the open space that made up the dining and living room, searching for Mary Beth. "Anyone home?"

A neon-pink note hung on the door with one word written in all caps. OUTSIDE.

Ashley groaned. If Mary Beth had taken off work to wait

for her outside, the day's situation might've been worse than Ashley realized. She pulled the heavy glass sliding door open. "Are you out here?"

"You know it."

She stepped out from the cool air-conditioning. "Don't make me go back into the heat." The deck faced the water, and pausing, Ashley drank in the view. The ocean was enough to soothe any bad day away.

"Over here." The top of Mary Beth's large-brimmed straw hat was visible from behind an Adirondack chair.

Ashley took off her heels and dropped her shoulder bag to the deck. "I don't think I've ever been so glad to hear your voice."

Mary Beth laughed and peeked over the chair's white-painted wooden slats. "Where else would I be when you're in the middle of the King Harbor gossip loop?"

"Ugh. Don't remind me." Ashley took the wooden chair next to Mary Beth. The slats warmed the backs of her thighs as she tilted her head toward the sun and adjusted her sunglasses. "Word travels fast."

"Yeah, word travels fast when you're trending on the internet." Mary Beth was never able to hide her amusement, even when she felt for the situation. Though if Ashley were on the other side, she *might* be able to see the hilarity. No one had died, and she'd come face-to-face with her ex-boyfriend on live television. It had the perfect makings of a rom-com.

"Even if the Blackthorne name and King Harbor weren't the most googled words today, the meme of your jaw dropping would've pulled me from work anyway."

Ashley groaned. "A meme?"

Mary Beth reached for her phone. "Several, actually."

"Don't show me. Let me pretend for now this wasn't a big thing."

Mary Beth leaned close. "Only after we discuss Phillip Blackthorne."

A red-hot streak of awareness slipped down her spine. "No, thank you."

"*No, thank you.* All the manners in the world aren't getting you out of this conversation," Mary Beth teased.

She pinched her eyes shut behind the dark lenses. "I don't want to talk about him."

"Suit yourself, but really, it's your loss." Mary Beth reached for a pitcher on the small deck table. "Because I made lemonade and am ready with my best listening ears."

"Rehashing the day—"

"Rehashing *Phillip*."

Her nose wrinkled as though his name stunk. "None of that is worth all the lemonade in King Harbor."

Mary Beth shrugged with a smile. "It is if I spiked it with Belvedere."

Ashley's eyebrow lifted at the mention of vodka. "We're having cocktails?"

"I am. *You* aren't having anything until I get some details."

Her brows dropped. "That's cruel."

"That's me. Mary Beth, the *Cruel One*."

Ashley reached for the lemonade anyway. Mary Beth playfully smacked her hand away. "Not a single delicious drop until you share."

She groaned. "You already saw everything on TV."

"On TMZ, actually. And Page Six. Oh, and a few dozen hot takes on social media."

"Ugh." She buried her head in her hands. "Really?"

"Really."

Ashley rubbed her temples then froze. "My mother's been calling."

"Ugh," Mary Beth added. "That's enough that I should just hand you the vodka."

"I haven't answered."

"No way," she said, reaffirming Ashley's decision to avoid

Mother at all costs. "I wouldn't either."

Her mother likely saw this as a Cartwright family public relations crisis. There were proper ways to do things— protocol. Surely a disastrous situation like this had been addressed in one of the Miss Manners books that lined her mother's office, even if Ashley couldn't recall a chapter about running into an ex on live TV while standing in the middle of a charity auction gone haywire.

"Okay, okay. Here." Mary Beth poured a glass of hard lemonade and handed it to Ashley. "I can't stand that deer-in-the-headlights look you have when you're worried what your mother will say."

She took the offered glass. "You *do* have a heart."

Her friend grinned. "Cheers."

"Cheers." Ashley took a long, approving sip.

"But my generous offer comes with strings," Mary Beth added.

"No—"

"You fill me in on every detail you've left out about Phillip Blackthorne."

She took another sip. "There's nothing to share."

Mary Beth scoffed, picking up her cell phone. A moment later, she handed Ashley the device.

Ashley's hand covered her mouth as her stomach fluttered. After taking a deep breath, she read the caption out loud. "That feeling when Cupid strikes." A second-long GIF cycled endlessly, replaying her split-second reaction when she first saw Phillip.

"Those are hearts in your eyes," Mary Beth coolly added and sipped her drink.

"Oh God."

"It gets better. Scroll down."

She didn't want to but couldn't help herself. Someone had stitched together clips of their faces, labeling each, "Shock. Anger. Happy. Horny." She blushed at that last word.

"Mary Beth... this is so bad."

"Honey, it's so true. Scroll a bit more. There's one where he's just looking at you."

"I don't want to see that!" But she scrolled anyway because that was a lie. Her heart thumped. The video zoomed in and out as he watched her with the reporter. She didn't need the captions to explain his possessive look. The brief clip made her stomach drop. "That's..."

Mary Beth fanned herself. "That's what the Laumet ladies would call *smitten*."

CHAPTER EIGHT

THE CELL PHONE rang shrilly from Ashley's purse and pulled her from the GIF of Phillip's eyes narrowing on her as he licked his bottom lip.

"Don't answer it," Mary Beth squeaked. "It could be her."

"You know that's not her ring." Long ago, Ashley had changed her mother's ringtone to a song fit for a horror movie.

"Yes, I know, but she's not stupid. She'll eventually call from an unknown number."

"Maybe it's Bitsy."

"Oh, joy," Mary Beth snickered. "She's not much better."

Ashley grabbed her purse and searched for her phone. "Bitsy could've been much worse today."

Mary Beth shrugged. "I suppose. You gave her free PR."

The call ended just as Ashley pulled her phone free. The screen displayed a missed call with a 202 area code. She held it up. "Not unknown."

"That's a Washington, DC number," Mary Beth added quickly.

Mary Beth would know, having been tempted to move to DC and take a job at an important accounting firm. Her decision, which wasn't fully made, was a roller coaster until Mary Beth decided to simply put the question of moving from King Harbor on hold.

"I don't know anyone from DC."

"Maybe it's one of your mother's people." Mary Beth

paused. "Be prepared to read a column about this in her magazine next month."

The phone rang again, and they both jumped. "Same number."

"Oh, that's her, and she's pissed," Mary Beth muttered.

Ashley wondered how many people read her mother's editorial columns. How many treated the magazine like gospel? Agatha Cartwright always knew the right thing to do. *Ha!* Most people probably thought the House of Cartwright was a gifted place of perfection; a wonderful home where correct sous-vide temperatures were as common knowledge as the perfect way to fold a fitted sheet.

In Ashley's house, the fitted sheets were all *nicely* rolled in squarish balls and shoved in the linen closet. She and Mary Beth had, so far, survived.

"Here goes nothing." Ashley steeled herself for Mother, picturing an action-item list written in black ink on thick cream cardstock. She imagined the bullet points detailed wording for handwritten note cards and phone calls to the donors. The action-item list most likely detailed the best way to extract herself from the fund-raiser and anything associated with Phillip Blackthorne. Ashley recalled the coldness from Mother when the woman had joked how Phillip was a blemish to the Blackthorne family name.

"Hello?"

"Hey, Ash." Phillip's voice crashed into her like a white-cap wave smashing against a jetty.

"Phillip?" Her stomach flipped. "Hey. Hi." Her eyes bugged as she looked at her best friend. "Hello…"

Mary Beth pulled her sunglasses to the tip of her nose and looked over the rim, mouthing, *"Phillip?"*

He laughed quietly. "Hey, hi, hello to you, too."

Her chin dropped. She was a mess. "I thought it was a bad connection."

"Right." He didn't sound convinced of her pathetic cover-up. "You ready to hash out a few ideas?"

Her jaw fell. "For the car show?"

"Well, yeah. Not a lot of time to make big changes."

"Oh, right. Wow, you work fast." She licked her lips, wondering where the steel-fortified version of herself had gone. This Ashley seemed more like a teenager with a crush. She counted to three and added a professional calmness when she said, "I'm ready to help. When works for you?"

"How about you come over now, and we'll—"

"*Now?*" she choked.

Mary Beth tipped off her chair, barely catching herself.

"Yeah," Phillip said. "Unless you're busy."

"No. I'm not." She had a meeting with The Laumet Society's insurance agent the next day, but other than that, spiked lemonades with her best friend were the only thing on the agenda. She'd never been to the Blackthorne estate before. The idea of heading over to *his place* intimidated her. She could envision it from pictures she'd seen in *Architectural Digest* and *New York Times* spreads, and that was a lot to take in. "I guess I'll see you soon."

They hung up. Ashley dropped the phone in her lap and stared straight ahead, nervous and giddy and… *nervous.*

"Did he invite you over?" Mary Beth scooted the heavy wood chair closer. "Never mind. That silly grin is answer enough."

Ashley covered her mouth, mumbling, "I'm supposed to hate him."

"Clearly." Mary Beth flipped her hand. "That's absolutely hatred dripping from you."

"I'm serious."

"You never told me the details behind your breakup, and I never pressed. But what I see right now is not an unhappy woman."

She blinked. "What am I?"

"Put that on your to-do list," Mary Beth quipped. "Seems

you need to figure that out."

She clutched her purse to her chest. "I don't think so."

"I do." Mary Beth laid her hand on Ashley's arm as she strangled the purse. "Go take a shower. Dab on a little perfume."

"*Mary Beth!*" Her thoughts scattered. "This is a work meeting."

Her best friend's lips twitched as though she had so much to say but didn't know where to start. Finally, she shook her head, adding, "No perfume, but you still need to shower. Ignore what I said and get to work."

"Right. Yeah." Ashley drew in a tight breath but was able to relax. Visiting the Blackthorne estate would be cool. Seeing Phillip would be a nonevent. She had to believe that about the man she wanted to hate but maybe, obviously, didn't.

CHAPTER NINE

B ROCK AND UNCLE Graham walked into the other side of
the large living room. Their hushed conversation faded
when they must've seen Phillip staring out the window. He
didn't bother to say hello to his uncle. A lecture loomed, and
Phillip would put it off as long as possible. Having his brother
tear into him today had already been enough. Little did either
of them know that the problem they were likely whispering
about was about to show up at their home.

Phillip's invitation for Ashley to meet him at the family
estate weighed heavily.

Or maybe it had left him even more confused than he'd
been earlier. It wasn't every day they invited those outside the
family's close network of friends for a social visit, as was
evident by Aunt Claire's birthday party. She'd wanted a
friends-only guest list, but true to the family's nature, business
associates and their attempt at a social-only gathering had
failed dramatically. Then again, Ashley's visit wasn't social.
They had business to address.

Phillip needed to focus on Ashley as a business associate.
Though the more he tried, the more he failed. Somehow
Ashley had cemented herself into his thoughts. He couldn't
close his eyes without replaying their time together—and that
was an unfair reason to have called her over for a working
meeting. Fair or not, he had to get her alone and figure out
why she preoccupied his thoughts.

He needed a shower before she arrived, preferably a cold

shower.

"Phillip, give me a minute." Graham crossed the living room.

"I was headed for a shower."

His uncle shook his head and eased onto the chair to the right of the couch. "I passed housekeeping a few minutes ago, bathroom cleaning tubs in hand."

His escape plan was foiled. Phillip hid a groan and took a seat to face his uncle, noting that Brock had quietly slipped away. "Guess I'll shower in a bit."

Graham ran his hand slowly through the graying salt-and-pepper hair as though searching for where to begin.

"About today," Phillip jumped in first. "It was a mistake but—"

His uncle dropped his hand, letting go of an exhausted sigh. "That was more than a mistake."

Phillip bit back explanations of failed brakes and wouldn't explain why he'd turned the morning into a golf cart joyride. Bringing up Aunt Claire had been the catalyst for the disaster earlier and wouldn't make this conversation go better.

"Public perception has been at an all-time high lately," Uncle Graham said. "We're up to our eyeballs in negotiations for a merger. Jason is dominating Hollywood. Ross walked away from racing. The Blackthorne name has been on the tip of the nation's tongue."

Of course his uncle didn't mention Aunt Claire leaving. Phillip was certain that interested more people than business deals. "I'm aware."

"More often than not, the coverage is positive."

Except... Phillip waited for the inevitable condemnation.

"Except when you pull stunts like today," Uncle Graham said. "You have to think."

"I was thinking."

"Then you have to think like a Blackthorne."

If thinking like a Blackthorne meant only thinking about

business, then he would never be able to meet his uncle's expectations. *Big surprise.* He hadn't met his father's either. He'd often wondered what Dad would have thought about the nonprofit and camp he'd created. Would either his dad or uncle be more receptive to it if Phillip had called it Camp Blackthorne instead of Camp Sunshine? Phillip gritted his teeth. "I'll work on that."

Uncle Graham leaned back as though their conversation had drained his energy. He pulled in a long breath and let it out as his gaze roamed the living room. Normally, Aunt Claire would be bustling throughout the house. Her lively cheer was infectious, and she turned what could be a designer's dream showcase of a house into a loving home.

Phillip missed his aunt. He didn't care for how empty and cavernous the estate felt without her presence. The look on his uncle's face said he felt that too. Phillip might've said that always thinking like a Blackthorne could be awfully lonely if he thought it would do any good with his stubborn uncle.

"Have a good day." Uncle Graham stood. "I'll be reviewing files in my office if anyone needs me."

The quiet surrounded Phillip again, but he couldn't sit still. He paced the windows that framed the bright living room. In any direction, he should've been able to find the kind of calm that only the ocean could offer. But the rolling waves failed to slow his increasing pulse. Being a Blackthorne wasn't a job. Perfection wasn't possible—and if he hadn't screwed up today, he wouldn't have run into Ashley—*literally.*

He grinned. She was one heart-stopping consequence. Phillip dropped to the couch and grabbed a magazine. Within a second, he tossed it aside, too impatient for her arrival to read.

Brock returned, giving Phillip a quick, questioning look. "What are you doing?"

"Nothing. What's it look like I'm doing?"

"Like you're doing nothing." Brock sucked his cheeks in

and continued to study Phillip.

"Then you're right." *As always.* But Phillip kept that part to himself.

"But with a dopey grin."

Phillip shrugged, trying the magazine again, and again casting it aside.

"Why do you look like that?" Brock pressed.

Phillip turned his palms up. "I hate to break it to you, Brother, but this is how I look." *Just like you.* They'd both been graced with their mother's dark eyes and hair.

"Huh… I'm going to run over to the Wharf," Brock said, mentioning the tourist-friendly shops. "Thought I'd grab a little something for Bitsy."

Slightly territorial regarding anything that stemmed from their morning, Phillip cocked his head. "Is that an invitation?"

"No."

"Good. I didn't want to go."

"It was an FYI," Brock added.

Phillip snorted. "FYI, I'm not your babysitter."

Brock shook his head. "Thank God you're no one's babysitter. The kid might not live through the day."

Phillip ignored the jab, throwing his own to his always Blackthorne-branded brother. "Be sure to find a gift with a barrel and thistle on it."

Brock smirked. "You're going to sit on your ass all day?"

"Versus what? Losing control of another golf cart? Creating headaches for the family?"

"You know what I meant."

Phillip straightened the pile of magazines on the coffee table. "Don't worry about me. I have my work for today cut out. Not all of us can fix things with gifts and schmoozing."

Brock snorted. "Funny."

"And true."

"What are you going to do?"

"Meet with Ashley. She's on her way here now. We're

going to hammer it out."

His brother's face froze. "Why?"

"Man, I can't win with you." Phillip straightened. "Do something. Don't do something. Which is it?"

"Why here?"

"Why not?" Phillip challenged, knowing he didn't have a good answer to the obvious question. Why was he bringing her over, alone?

Brock took his glasses off and pinched the bridge of his nose. "You've got to be kidding me."

Phillip glared up but said nothing.

He shook his head, cleaned his glasses, and replaced them. "I can't believe you'd make a move on her after what you did today."

Phillip scowled. "I'm not making a move on her. Grow up."

"Grow up is my advice for you." Brock strode across the living room. The sun steamed from behind the westward window and framed him, making him appear as if he were about to dispense heavenly knowledge. "Don't do whatever you're thinking about doing."

"Don't do whatever I'm thinking about doing?" Phillip stood. "Is your opinion of me that low? That I'm only interested in one thing when it comes to her?"

"Prove me wrong," Brock challenged.

"I don't need to prove anything to you." Phillip's jaw ticked. He checked his watch. "The only thing I need to do is take a shower."

Brock's eyebrow crooked. "Housekeeping just finished in my suite and headed into yours."

The summer's stickiness clung to his skin. It wouldn't take Ashley too long to arrive. He checked his watch again. He might have time to wait out Pam.

"Use my bathroom," Brock said. "You can't meet with Ashley—or anyone—looking like you do."

"Always on brand." But Phillip decided that using Brock's bathroom was a good idea. "But okay. Thanks." Then he pretended to smooth a hand over his nonexistent beard. "Maybe take your own advice too. I don't remember adding a woolly mammoth to the brand packaging."

"Funny."

"I thought so." Phillip walked toward the back stairs with a spring in his step. Ashley would be there soon and—a magazine whooshed across the room and smacked his shoulder. He turned to his brother. "So, you're going for a caveman, not a woolly mammoth? Throwing things clears that up."

"Earlier today…" Brock overlooked the joke and crossed his arms. "When I said that I didn't see how you and Ashley would last, I meant when we were at Harvard."

Caught off guard, Phillip waited to see where Brock would take the conversation.

"If you're not bringing her over to make a move—"

"I'm not," Phillip growled.

Brock dropped his arms and shoved his hands into his pockets. "How would you know unless the opportunity presented itself?"

Subconsciously, wasn't that why Phillip had invited her over? Being near her and having an agenda weren't the same. "Back off, Brock."

"She's a great person."

Earlier, Phillip had been jealous of their interactions. Now he didn't know who Brock was trying to protect. "You've already hammered that point."

The corners of Brock's gaze tightened behind his glasses. "If you're after something more than a fling with her—"

"It's a *working* meeting. What are you missing?"

He met Phillip's eyes. "Then I wish you the best of luck."

CHAPTER TEN

"GOOD AFTERNOON, MISS Cartwright." The woman who answered the door beckoned Ashley in.

"Thank you." Ashley stepped inside the breathtaking foyer. If she'd thought the lush gardens outside would leave her breathless, she had another think coming with the expansive entryway. "And please." She extended her hand. "I'm Ashley."

"Nice to meet you, Ashley. I'm Pam." Pam offered to take her purse.

Ashley clung to her bag like it was her security blanket.

"I believe Phillip is waiting for you in the living room."

She followed Pam as they walked down the hall.

But he wasn't in the living room when they arrived. "I can wait here." She didn't mind the opportunity to take in the expansive oceanfront through the picture windows. Luscious green and flowering gardens met the rocky edge of an incline that led to the white sand beach.

"Can I get you a drink?" Pam asked. "Water? A whisky?"

"No, thank you. I'm fine." Her nerves had her so rattled that a drink might shake in her hand.

"Then I'll let Phillip know that you're here."

Brock entered, greeting her with a friendly hello, and adding, "I told Phillip that Ashley arrived."

"Then my work here is done." Pam left the way they'd come in.

"The Blackthorne estate is so much more than I could

have imagined." Ashley gestured to the view. "It's just… breathtaking."

"There's nothing I'd rather do than tell you about its history." Brock took a deep breath and let it out slowly, then cautiously added, "But I understand you have a meeting."

"I do." She grinned, knowing Brock to be the consummate family storyteller.

He gestured toward a far hallway. "Phillip said something about getting straight to business."

"All business," she said, then regretted her unconvincing tone. Brock was a business partner, and after everything he'd seen between her and Phillip today, she needed to ensure he saw her as a professional.

"If you head upstairs to meet him now, we might find time to regale you with family history later."

"Upstairs?" That sounded far from professional, and her nerves skittered at the thought of wandering the estate alone. "I can wait." But it seemed as though Brock would rather she not. Uncomfortable, she changed the subject. "I didn't have a moment to say thank you for how you handled everything. Especially Lori."

"It comes with the job."

She smoothed her skirt. "Yes, but you made the television spot… salvageable."

His eyebrow arched as he chuckled. "We're calling that salvageable?"

She blushed. "Yes, well, except the confusion at the end." And the beginning. And she couldn't forget the part in the middle. Brock watched her as though he were trying to read her mind. "Anyhow, thanks for keeping a handle on the reporter."

He grinned. "Sorry I wasn't able to keep a handle on the rest."

"Oh no." She thought of the memes, GIFs, and internet chatter. "You saw that?"

His grin broke into laughter. "I was there in person but apparently oblivious to a few things."

A hot blush heated her cheeks. "There wasn't anything to see."

"Uh-huh. Phillip said the same thing." Brock checked his pocket for his wallet and keys. "I'm headed to the Wharf in search of something for Bitsy."

"You don't have to do that. She's the happiest I've ever seen her."

"Sometimes any press is good press, but a gift never hurts." Brock gestured toward the far hallway. "Upstairs. Third door on the right. Can't miss him."

Then Brock left, and Ashley was alone in the great hall of a living room. It shouldn't have been awkward. There wasn't even another person to be awkward in front of. But she fidgeted, smoothing her skirt and readjusting her purse.

The seconds seemed like hours, and finally, Ashley was unable to wait anymore. Getting their visit over with was best anyway. She wandered down the hall, inching deeper into the stunning home. "Hello?"

No one answered, and she slowly made her way to where Brock directed her. One thing after another caught her eye. Pictures and portraits hung on the walls. Framed historic maps of Scotland and Maine lined the walls as she inched up the stairs. "Hello?"

The giant house hummed with a silence that made her feel like she'd sneaked in. There weren't familiar sounds. There weren't *any* sounds.

The first door on her right was slightly ajar. She studied the award-winning design of the room through the crack, nudging it wider to take in the stunning views and vaulted ceilings.

Curious, she moved to the second door. It wasn't ajar but wasn't completely shut. She inched it open, wondering what she would find—

The door swung open, and a warm, damp chest barreled into her. Ashley stumbled back, her heels doing her no favors as she toppled—almost. She was trapped in the arms of a bare-chested man. *Phillip.*

"Oh!" She jerked away, and her cheek slapped into his muscular chest. Phillip regained his footing, still holding her, then let her wriggle away. "I'm so—" She choked. Phillip wore only a towel. "Sorry…" A furious blush washed over her. Another apology was hot on the last one's trail when it caught in her throat.

Phillip eased back. "Are you okay?"

Not at all. She blinked and stared. Water droplets clung to his skin. The definition of his pectoral muscles carved themselves into her memory, ensuring that she would never forget this moment. Unable to stop her roaming gaze, she followed the dark smattering of chest hair that thinned closer to his abdomen. Water trailed down his stomach, sliding over the ridges of taut skin, and disappeared into the towel wrapped dangerously low over his hips.

"We keep crashing into each other today," he said as though he weren't dripping wet and nearly naked.

Her chin jerked up. Ashley remembered to breathe, choking on a gasp before a semi-erratic pattern of breaths returned. Gathering enough nerve to look him in the eye, she almost ran at the sight of Phillip's impish grin.

"You're…" She couldn't figure out what to say. "In a towel."

His grin grew into one that packed far more heat, making it apparent that he enjoyed what he'd seen: her drinking him in. "That obvious?"

She jerked from him, retreating until her back bumped against the wall. His lips twitched.

"I didn't—I mean… I wasn't." Her tongue twisted as her hands slapped across her eyes, shielding the view. "Your brother said to come up here."

Phillip made a curious noise. Ashley prayed for another set of hands to cover her ears.

"I'm running behind," he said. "Give me a minute."

"Of course." She spun to face the wall, still covering her eyes. Maybe she could melt into it. If there was ever time for a superpower, walking through walls would work well at that moment. "Or I can just go."

His footsteps padded away as he laughed quietly. "You've seen me with less."

Ashley thumped her hand-covered head against the wall. "I'm so, so sorry."

ONE FOOT IN *front of the other.* That was all Phillip could think until he escaped behind the closed door. His next breath lodged in his throat. His bedroom seemed smaller and warmer than it should. *He* was warmer—no, he was burning up. Arousal danced through his veins. It punched in time with his pulse. The memory of her face, her *shock*, with hungry eyes and parted lips, stained his vision and colored his thoughts.

He'd barely had a rational moment to think since his jealousy spiked and he'd invited her over, wanting to be with her alone. But now that he'd seen that look on her face, he wanted a whole lot more than to test the waters with a flirtatious game while they did their work. He wanted to see her desire again, which meant he needed to control his reactions to her.

Easier said than done. Tension still choked him. He pulled a deep breath and dropped the towel. Cool air slid over his naked hips and groin and did little to quell the growing from deep within.

He flipped a wall switch, and the overhead fan silently stirred the air, failing to cool the hold she had on his thoughts as he crossed the room. Helpless to them, Phillip fell face-first onto the mattress.

Teasing her shouldn't be so fun. Hurt should be his only reaction when faced with the pain from the past. Too bad that hurt didn't come. Time had allowed his heart to forgive and forget.

The overhead fan found its cruising speed. Lazy circles blew over his shower-dampened skin. Moisture wicked away, and he rolled over. "Get a grip."

Again, easier said than done. Frustrated, he pushed off the bed and stalked to his dresser. His reflection didn't look wary of her. He glared at the mirror. "Be careful."

But of what? Worrying about getting hurt meant that he wanted to test the waters, knowing full well he couldn't handle a meaningless fling with Ashley.

Wow. Phillip surprised himself. But the man in the mirror wasn't worried. He was grinning as though he'd discovered the meaning of life.

He turned, trying to juggle his thoughts. Just because he wanted her back didn't mean that he would blindly charge forward and count on their chemistry to reignite what had been a white-hot love. He was older and wiser than the punk he'd been in college. That had to count for something. Phillip rubbed his hands into his hair, deciding to take it slow, then wondering how Ashley had changed. He didn't know but wanted to find out—and he would have to prove to her that he was a better version of the man she'd loved and left.

"After the car show," he told himself. All he needed was a plan.

CHAPTER ELEVEN

HOLY GREEK GODS, that man was sex on a stick. Ashley wasn't sure what to do. When she closed her eyes, her mind went into overdrive, recalling how they'd collided. If she kept her eyes open... well, she had nearly the same thoughts.

"Pull it together," she silently ordered then searched for a few good reasons to forget what she'd just seen. The human body was nothing new, Ashley reminded herself. But no amount of pep talk or lecture calmed her rush of excitement and memories. The more she tried to ignore the crackling awareness that hung in the air, the more she pictured Phillip's bare chest and that towel that hung dangerously low.

College Phillip had been hot. But this Phillip?

The door clicked open. Her breath caught once again, and she flushed, hot with her wandering thoughts.

"Safely dressed." Phillip stepped into the hall, wearing a well-fitted shirt and casual shorts.

Dressed, not dressed. She didn't care because she could see a maturity and hunger in his dark eyes. Passing time and lessons learned the hard way seemed to have hardened him. Her heart fluttered when his reserved gaze held her captive.

"Better now?" he asked.

"Much. All's forgotten." *Lies!* Nothing would erase the permanent image of a half-naked Phillip ready to catch her.

He shoved his hands into his pockets, keeping his taunting amusement and sarcasm at bay. "Great."

Ashley fumbled for what to say, worried that if she said

too much, he would know the truth: He was now officially fodder for her daydreams.

"Let's get to work." He was as cool as an ice-cold Moxie and gave her a wide berth as he walked around her then lifted a hand toward the stairs she'd come up. "We can sit down in the living room."

That seemed safe enough. She would have no choice but to focus on work. "Okay."

"Though if Nana walks in and challenges you to a drinking game, just say no."

Ashley blanched. "Okay."

Phillip seemed to consider additional interruptions. "Or if Devlin and Hannah come by again, don't listen to anything they say."

"Meaning what?"

"Never mind." He turned toward his bedroom, maybe considering their privacy, but shook his head. "We can talk and walk on the beach."

The beach would work. She couldn't go near his bedroom, but Ashley paused and lifted her high-heel-clad foot. "I left my walking shoes at home."

He grinned. "Good thing you stumbled my way."

"Why?"

"If you don't know how to take your shoes off and walk along the beach, then you're worse off than I'd guessed."

She laughed, rolling her eyes. "I can take my shoes off."

"Then let's go, beautiful."

Her heart skipped. "Now?"

"We can stand here in the hall for a few minutes if it'd make you feel more comfortable."

She rolled her eyes.

"Watch." He kicked off his leather sandals and nudged his head toward the stairs. "That's how it's done."

"Ha, ha, funny guy. I'll take them off downstairs, by the door."

He raised a shoulder. "Suit yourself."

There was nothing intimate about shedding her shoes, yet doing so outside his bedroom door made her feel too exposed, which filled her to the brim with wild butterflies. "Thank you."

She fell into stride with him as they moved down the stairs. Their elbows brushed, and her giddy butterflies flipped along with her stomach. But as much as she enjoyed the unintentional touch, she hated her reaction to the man. They needed distance and boundaries, or she would lose her mind.

Phillip opened the door leading outside then gave her a careful once-over. "Are you okay?"

Not a chance. An emotional civil war battled inside her. She longed for the sparks that came from their familiar closeness as much as she wanted to pull away and guard her heart. Ashley tottered in her heels, confused and scared to be alone on the beach with him.

Phillip locked his gaze on her, and the moment felt as though he wanted to read her mind. Her next breath stalled.

"You can do it," he joked. "Promise."

That pulled her back to reality. Phillip didn't want to see into her thoughts. He wanted to get under her skin. "I know I can do it." With deliberate exaggeration, she removed her heels, dropping a few inches shorter, and picked them up. Her mother's voice chimed at the back of her mind with a much-shared Coco Chanel quote. "Keep your heels, head, and standards high."

Or what? She'd often bit back the question. God forbid anyone question Agatha Cartwright, especially when she was channeling Coco Channel. The world of style and beauty might implode.

Ashley squared her shoulders and held her head up. "Lead the way."

"You can leave all that if you want." He glanced at her shoes and purse.

Her bag was draped protectively across her shoulders, and she held her shoes like a set of daggers. Ashley hesitated. Leaving her shoes would be okay. Her purse, on the other hand… Leaving that would be akin to removing her armor. She'd have nothing to hide behind.

"Or not. Do what you want." He opened the door.

The warm, salty air rolled in and offered comfort. Walking on the beach with Phillip was not unlike walking on the beach anywhere else in King Harbor. The waves would roll in. The birds would dance on the sand. All would be normal, not necessitating her armor.

Slowly, she lowered her bag until it dangled in her fingers. Maybe she would take her cell phone. Of course she would need her sunglasses. But the bag dropped to the beautiful wood floor.

"No one will take it." He winked and nudged her bag to the wall with his bare foot.

No matter what her mother had always said, accessories were not her weapons. Also, Phillip wasn't a bad guy. She didn't need to be scared of him. That was only what Mother had said.

She glanced at him waiting expectantly for her to walk out the door. He was the only person who'd ever peeled back her layers. She'd almost let him get close enough to figure out what had happened before. *Terrifying.*

He stepped out the back door, leaving it open for the breeze to tempt her with a promise of the sun. Wisps of the warm afternoon collided with the air-conditioning. The seesawing temperatures mirrored her internal chaos. The outdoors—and Phillip—called to her. Ashley dropped her shoes next to her bag and rushed onto the deck. "Wait for me."

CHAPTER TWELVE

"I'M COMING." ASHLEY rushed to catch up with Phillip. He'd crossed the deck and descended the long, winding stairs. She wanted to rush but the view forced her to slow down. On either side of the stairs, lush gardens and rolling greens framed the private beach that waited ahead.

The sand glimmered even though the sun had started to sink westward in the bright-blue sky. The tranquility called to her for a peace that she hadn't realized she needed, and Ashley floated down the final steps onto the beach.

"Ouch." The sandy beach was beautiful, but it was also hotter than Hades on vacation. Ashley pranced more than she walked, quickly shuffling toward Phillip and the damp sand from the lowering tide.

Phillip waited, amused, along the shoreline, but Ashley kept trucking until the bottom of her feet were submerged by a rolling wave.

She wriggled her toes in the wet sand as the wave pulled away. "Sandals next time."

"Next time." He laughed.

A breeze picked up, sweeping her hair from her shoulders and tangling it in the wind. Her dress billowed, and the silky fabric blew against her legs. Ashley drank in a deep breath, feeling herself relax. It was impossible to hold on to worries and stress at the beach. She dropped her head back to soak in the sun and wind.

After a long moment of simply existing in the sun, she

opened her eyes to Phillip. "It was a good idea to come out here."

A rolling wave washed over their feet. Two shorebirds flitted ahead of them.

Phillip stood close. Their arms brushed like before, but instead of the fiery intensity from earlier, a quiet fulfillment washed over her. She leaned against his arm then into his chest. Without a word of interruption, he wrapped her to him. The world swayed. Ashley lost herself in him, melting into memories and muscles. The years dissolved, and time slowed as her eyes shut, her cheek resting against his chest.

Ca-caw. The wings of a shorebird flapped hard as it took flight and cut close overhead as it squawked again.

She jerked away. Surprise caught in her throat, and embarrassment flooded from the depths of her unguarded heart.

"I'm sorry." A blush scorched her skin. "I, uh... didn't meant to..." Curl into him? Yes, she had, craving that serene intoxication his arms offered. "I'm sorry."

The corners of his eyes tightened. He rolled his bottom lip into his mouth. She couldn't read his expression and couldn't forget how he'd held on to her. They had been lost, together, in each other, and she simply couldn't let that happen.

Phillip walked ahead. Ashley watched as their distance grew. He didn't look over his shoulder, and again, she didn't know what to say. Small talk would feel forced, and she was too distracted to focus on work.

She jogged through a receding wave until they were side by side again. Small talk didn't surface. Nothing did. Ashley wondered if they should talk about them, about what had just happened, or whatever had happened years ago. She'd never said she was sorry. At the time, she'd been drowning in indignation and bad advice. What would her apology sound like now?

Ashley bit her lip and judged herself. The college kid that had been trying to live up to her mother's expectations, to gain anything that could pass as approval. At the time, Ashley had believed the breakup was warranted. Her regret lay in *how* she'd ended the relationship.

But this Ashley? The one walking beachside, relaxing into his arms? Her guilt spread, slowly unfurling like a coil. She'd never accepted her share of the blame. Goat crap and an overbearing mother weren't solid excuses for the how and when of their breakup. She wanted to say, "*Phillip, it wasn't all you.*" But she wouldn't waste a poor justification as an excuse for a weak apology. She could do better.

Phillip cleared his throat. "Housekeeping was in my bedroom."

"What?" She blinked then shielded her eyes from the sun, finally having enough guts to look him in the face.

"Earlier. That's why I was in Brock's room."

"Oh!" Ashley breathed easier at the change of subject. "You don't have to explain why you were someplace in your own home."

"I know," he added thoughtfully. "We'd had a pretty strong back-and-forth earlier."

"About what?"

He raised an eyebrow. "You."

"Oh." Suddenly, it didn't feel like the topic had changed that much. "Well, whatever that was about, everything seemed fine when he told me where to find you."

"I was in the shower."

Her cheeks heated. "Yeah. I know."

Phillip laughed it off, letting the conversation disappear, though he stayed lost in thought. She took what he'd said, playing with the words like a jigsaw puzzle, wondering what he hadn't said. Then it hit her. Was Brock playing matchmaker again? No. He would never. But then why had he pointed her toward Phillip in the shower? Perhaps he was testing them, or better yet, maybe he wanted whatever would happen between her and Phillip to happen earlier rather than later.

"Even if Brock had been up to something…" she said.

He harrumphed. "Something."

She blushed again but would make her point. "Even if he

was, he couldn't have anticipated our…"

"Crash?"

She laughed. "Good word for it, and besides, I was… wandering."

Phillip's eyebrow arched.

"Wandering," she repeated, wondering if ambling would have been a better explanation. Either word was easier to admit rather than the tiny bit of snooping and spying she'd done.

"What does that mean?"

"I don't know. I was taking it all in."

He laughed. "You're making that face."

"What face? I didn't make a face." One of her many talents was the ability to conceal her reactions… from everyone but Phillip. That was a long-forgotten fact that she now knew to be all too true.

"Yeah, you did, beautiful."

Her heart skipped like a stone thrown across the water. "Don't call me that." Because she liked it too much.

Amusement lightened his features. "That's the face where there's way more to the story—"

"You're seeing things."

"—than you're letting on," he finished.

Her forehead furrowed. How did he know her so well? She stammered to explain her wandering.

"Are you going to tell me?" he asked. "Or I could guess. You were wandering around the estate—"

"Stop." Ashley balked. "Your ability to read people is irritating."

"My ability to read you."

Her stomach bottomed. "It's irritating." It irked her in ways she didn't know were possible. She wanted to storm away or wrap her hands around his throat, or better yet, wrap herself to him, and she nearly swooned at the idea of a kiss. Instead of strangling or kissing, she lowered her voice and controlled her words with calm precision. "There's not. I'm a wandering ambler. End of the story."

"Sure." Phillip's mouth quirked, making it evident that the subject hadn't been dropped. It was only on mute.

She rolled her eyes, irritated that her poker face had gone away with her nerves of steel. They'd run off together, maybe to New Brunswick or Quebec, somewhere that would serve cocktails and celebrity gossip that didn't revolve around anyone she knew.

The silence made her skin crawl. It seemed as if even the shorebirds and the waves were quiet, waiting until she explained herself. "I'm partially to blame for our little run-in earlier."

He hummed like a detective. "How's that?"

Good question. *I was snooping...* "I was curious—"

"That's not new." Phillip paused to face her and crossed his arms, his universal signal that he was giving his full attention.

That wasn't what she needed. "I wanted to know what the rooms looked like, and the first door wasn't closed. I peeked."

His eyebrow arched, and his lips twitched.

"The next one. It was slightly open, and..." She shrugged and feigned as much nonchalance as she could muster. "We collided."

His dancing eyes brightened, and his deep-barreled laughter broke as a wave crashed against the backs of her legs. At least the silence was gone.

Finally, he teased, "Guess that'll teach you."

Her eyes rolled. "Give me a break." A strong wave smacked her from behind, and her balance faltered. She grabbed her skirt, failing to keep the fabric from the water as she searched for her footing.

Phillip lifted her from the water. The effortless move made her feel as if she could fly, then made her head spin, locked in his arms.

The wind blew her hair, drawing a curtain around their faces as he slowly set her down.

"Rogue wave," he said, not taking his hands from under her arms.

Wet fabric stuck to the backs of her thighs. Her hands slid down his chest, and she felt a heat deep within. Carefully, she removed her palms from his chest. The lack of contact revived an ache she couldn't quite forget. Her internal war reignited. Wanting what she let go of. Hating how that made her feel. Another wave came again, though this time with far less power. Still, she used it as an excuse to step away.

He caught her arm, and she swallowed hard. One of them had to say something.

But each, apparently, were lost as to what they should do, so they didn't. She backed another protective step away from their pull, fearing their attraction of polar opposites. College mistakes wouldn't be the only problem if she let their paradoxical chemistry call the shots. Ashley couldn't let down The Laumet Society. She wouldn't embarrass herself with a business partner like Brock Blackthorne. And her mother... She could never give Mother another chance to point out the flaws of a good man.

Her hand pressed to the small of her throat. "I can't do this."

"Do what?"

This. Us. Tears burned behind her eyes. She *hadn't* broken up with Phillip only because of a stupid goat or because he hadn't fit into the cookie-cutter image that her mother had raised her to see as love. Ashley ended things with him because he was irresponsible and selfish. He lacked foresight of the future, and... and... none of her reasons had ever been true. She'd always known that, but they were too different, doomed to fail. "I have to go."

She spun. Again, he caught her. Her chin snapped up. "Let me go!"

"I have no intention of letting you run away this time." Though he let go of her arm. "You have questions to answer. That much you owe me."

Her lips trembled.

"But..." He eased back, giving her room. "I won't make you deal with this now."

"I don't know what you're talking about." *Lies again!*

Instead of exposing the truth, she turned the conversation—and his intentions—around. "Why did you ask me to come here?"

He took too long to come up with an honest answer. An ache split her heart. She didn't know why. But anything involving Phillip was always a mistake.

"I always wondered if you'd end up like your mother or not."

Ashley gasped. His conversation turnabout hit far closer to the truth and made her ill.

He continued. "I remember when the queen of all things home and garden had tapped you to rule her fiefdom one day."

Ashley clenched her fists but didn't have this fight in her, and her hands loosened. "Please don't compare me to her."

Phillip stepped closer, and with another hill of her roller coaster, she desperately missed how his arms could make the rest of the world disappear.

"What happened? Why aren't you on the throne?" he asked.

Phillip had happened. Losing him had happened. Losing her way, the one she loved, losing everything because she couldn't be true to herself, that had all happened! Then everything had changed. Her eyes slipped shut, and a tear slipped free. She wondered how to explain any of it and couldn't figure out a way to share without hurting both of them again. Ashley wiped the rogue tear away and tamped down the truth.

They didn't touch, but as he towered over her, Ashley wished for what she couldn't have. *Him.*

"Tell me the truth," he demanded. "At least on that."

He had no idea it was all the same thing. The hate she claimed for him was really aimed at herself, and knowing that, she ran away.

CHAPTER THIRTEEN

P HILLIP SQUINTED AS the morning sun shined through the cloudy sky. He'd relished the overcast weather while pummeling baseballs in the batting cages at Harbor Park but decided, as he slid his sunglasses into place, the sun would only help.

The pitching machine threw another ball. He concentrated for the swing, letting the nearby children that played and laughed in the distance slip away.

Crack.

That could've been a grand freakin' slam, but again, it didn't help. He cursed to himself as the pitching machine readied another ball. Phillip gripped the bat, wondering when he would hit enough balls to release his aggravation that had compounded since Ashley ran off the beach the day before.

I let her go. A baseball whizzed by Phillip's head without him taking a swing. *Let her go just like I did before.*

The mechanical crank of the pitching machine didn't stop because his mind was hopscotching between the present and past. He repositioned his grip on the Louisville Slugger as he listened to the repetitive machine crank another ball into position.

The pitching machine's hum held his focus. He needed the hit and craved the impact, wanting to hear the collision between bat and ball and feel that resounding crack. Sooner or later, it would help clear his mind.

The pitch barreled down the lane. His eyes narrowed, and

Phillip swung. *Crack.* The impact offered sweet relief, though it was fleeting. His muscles ached. Sweat beaded on the back of his neck and clung to his shirt.

The robotic crank readied another ball, but the mechanical hum died. The automatic pitching arm whined down until it came to a rest. Exhausted and no less aggravated, Phillip dropped his grip on the Slugger and turned.

Devlin stepped from behind a partition. "Nana said I'd find you here."

Phillip wiped his forehead with his shirt. "Nana?" He ran a hand through his hair then exchanged the bat for a bottle of water, sucking several gulps down.

"She was tending to her garden when she saw you storm out with the bat."

Nana missed nothing. Somehow, she had eyes everywhere. Phillip could only wish to be as lively as she was when he got to her age. "If you wanted to hit balls, you could've called."

Devlin took one of the bats that lined the lane wall, tossed it over his shoulder with ease, and swung through with perfect form. "I don't want to hit balls."

Phillip cut his gaze down the lane and took another gulp from his water bottle.

"I doubt you would've answered anyway."

He capped the bottle. "Then why are you here?"

Devlin rested the bat over his shoulder. "We gave you grief over the accident and Ashley."

"I was there, but thanks for the reminder."

"No one's brought up the Ferrari, huh?"

Phillip gave a hard glare to his cousin, which failed to force a subject change, then shrugged. "Huh is right."

"We know that car—"

He held up his hand. "No one knows anything about that car."

The corner of Devlin's eyes tightened. "Uncle Mark—"

"Today's not the day to talk about my dad. Okay?"

Devlin rolled his lips together and backed against the lane partition. "Have you ever noticed that we're more alike than not?"

Phillip rubbed the back of his neck. He'd come to the cages to let go of tension, only to have it multiply. "We're all alike."

"Ha." Devlin grinned. "Now I know you're saying whatever to get me to leave."

Phillip chuckled. "Okay. Me and Brock? Nothing alike."

"Me and Jason?" Devlin mimicked a phone to his ear. "Not always alike. But you and me? We aren't working out of the corporate headquarters."

"I'd lose my mind."

"I almost did." Devlin laughed. "But I found my place on the water."

"Like I did with the camp."

"Dedicating your life to nonprofit work says a lot."

"Yeah, it says that I don't fit in the family mold." Phillip meant to sound angry, but he was exhausted. He leaned against the lane partition next to his cousin, and thankfully, Devlin let the conversation die.

Phillip watched the remaining low-hanging clouds, letting his thoughts drift from Ashley to the Ferrari. Both made his throat dry. He swiped the water bottle, knowing it wouldn't help, but guzzled the last few ounces anyway.

Devlin watched him finish the water and toss the bottle onto his gear bag. "You can tell her no."

"The Ferrari?" Phillip shook his head. "I don't want to."

"Really?"

"It's just a car."

"Yeah." Devlin snorted. "Like we drink any old whisky—you're out here beating the hell out of baseballs for no reason."

"Not over the car."

Devlin lifted his eyebrow. "Over Ashley?"

Yes—but no. "Over..." He shrugged. "Not doing what I should when I'm supposed to."

Devlin inhaled deeply and cocked his head. "That's deep."

Phillip snorted. "Tell me about it." But that was his ongoing problem. He'd let her leave yesterday without forcing a conversation. In college, he should've chased after her instead of letting his pride keep him away. Even when he was a kid, Phillip was up to his eyeballs in everything he wasn't supposed to do. That was what had landed him in wilderness camp. If he'd only behaved like the rest of the world wanted him to, his parents would still be alive.

An overbearing silence thundered as though his personal dark cloud threatened a storm over his head.

"We both know what that car means to me." He swallowed hard and lowered his voice. "What I didn't know"—he pressed the heel of his palm to the bat knob—"was what Ashley meant to me."

THERE WERE FEW times that Ashley had been more appreciative of Mary Beth's knack with numbers than that morning. One day, she would convince her best friend to take the big-shot job in DC, but for now, she appreciated Mary Beth doing her another countless favor.

"Hand me that one." Mary Beth pointed with her fork.

"The syrup or the paperwork?"

"I have more than enough syrup."

"That's not possible." Ashley eyed the mountain of paperwork stacked in neatly organized piles on the dining room table, thanks to Mary Beth. She passed the papers and watched her best friend polish off the last of her pancakes before paging through the pile.

"I never thought I'd be grateful for Bitsy." Mary Beth highlighted several lines with a yellow marker. "But I am."

Bitsy had provided everything Ashley needed for the meeting with The Laumet Society's insurance agent, Mr. Van de Molen.

Deductibles? That had seemed easy enough. But then the nitty-gritty fine print turned to gibberish. Actual cost versus replacement costs, value versus price. Ashley had a fantastic education, but general nonprofit liability clauses and exceptions made her head spin.

Mary Beth, on the other hand, found that stuff fun. She inhaled what was covered, what was not, deductibles, caps, and more terms and conditions than Ashley could shake a pancake at.

"The Laumet Society has really great coverage," Mary Beth added, handing Ashley a form. "This is going to be easy."

"Uh-huh." Ashley finished chewing and read the header. *Itemized Donation List.* "I suppose that's relative."

Mary Beth snorted. "Then we better get to work."

Two hours, Ashley was as well-versed in what they'd lost as she could be, and Mary Beth had earned more favors than Ashley could ever pay back.

The doorbell rang, and her stomach dropped. She couldn't figure out why her nerves had been so anxious—well, she had a small clue that she hadn't voiced out loud yet. Insurance meant litigation. Litigation against the Blackthornes meant problems. Their lawyers had lawyers, and the pool of funds to pay monstrous hourly wages was never-ending. In theory, or at least in her imagination, the charity fund-raiser had the ability to bankrupt The Laumet Society, particularly since she'd run from the Blackthorne who seemed intent on pushing her buttons.

CHAPTER FOURTEEN

THE VAULT SHOULD'VE been a safe place. Phillip had spent countless hours in the bar. It was an extension of his family, much like the distillery around back. But today, with a scheduled appointment in a public place with Ashley, the familiar dark-paneled walls lined with bottles offered no comfort. He scanned the room and saw her seated at a side table with a drink and notebook at hand. Her hair was pulled into a high ponytail, giving Phillip a look at her long neck. She had a sweet spot behind her ear and along her shoulder. Before he could stop the memory of conjuring goose bumps with the slide of his lips, he grinned.

But that wasn't why they were there. He took a long breath and ambled across the Vault. His hand trailed the top of her high-back barstool chair as he offered a hello and took the chair across the small table. He'd resolved to have a professional meeting. Nothing would be awkward. His hands would stay on his side of the table. His mind would focus on the charity work. Phillip wouldn't flirt or antagonize her. They wouldn't bicker. And if he prayed hard enough, he wouldn't think about giving her goose bumps for the remainder of their meeting.

"Thanks for meeting me." Ashley tucked her elbows at her side, hiding her hands under the table.

"A public place seemed best."

Her lips parted, and her long eyelashes fluttered as she blinked. Phillip hadn't made it more than ten seconds into the conversation before making her react.

"I guess this is as legitimate of a place to work as you can manage," she said.

He held up his hands. "The Vault isn't to your liking?"

"You know what I mean."

"Actually, no, beautiful. I don't know what you mean. Alone at my home didn't work well for you." Damn, he did it again. But it was the truth. She was the living, breathing definition of beautiful.

Her cheeks pinked.

"I meant *Ashley*."

"And I thought we'd meet at an office, a boardroom."

"Ah." He eased into the chair and leaned back, unable to help himself. "I thought you didn't want to be alone with me."

She glared. "Stop."

"Even if I could read your mind, it'd be a mix of U-turns and—"

"Stop," she repeated. Her nostrils flared as she gave a quick headshake. "Wait. Can we start over? Please?"

Phillip folded his arms. "You can't call for a new take if you didn't like the first round."

The server arrived, greeting him by name and bringing him his usual—Blackthorne Gold. A tense beat passed, and he stared at the whisky.

Ashley's sigh shattered his lost thoughts. He lifted his chin, catching her lips squeezed together. "I walked in here, telling myself not to act like a jackass."

"Why are we fighting?"

There were a lot of answers he could give, but instead, he sipped the whisky and took his time setting down the glass. "The easiest answer is because you ran off from the beach."

"What's the hardest answer?" she asked.

Phillip rolled his bottom lip into his mouth and struggled to keep the truth to himself. They were fighting because, if they didn't, he would kiss her. If he kissed her, he would touch her. Things would move quickly. He would have to have her. Fighting was the only way he'd figured out how to take things slow.

But after thinking of what would happen, when one thing would lead to the next and the next, until he had her naked in his arms... Phillip grumbled. "You're right. We should start over."

She grinned. "Thank you."

He snickered, silently admitting that agreeing with Ashley hadn't cleared his thoughts, and hoped a good-natured joke would ease his tension. "Where do we start?" He leaned off the chair. "Should I walk in again? Just say hello?"

"We can pick it up from here," she said, thankfully not taking him for an ass. "But no small talk."

He settled back into his seat. "I can do that. Jump right into the car show."

"I mean, I'm not a dictator. It doesn't all have to be about work." She fidgeted. "I just meant that we shouldn't bother with those dumb questions that people feel they need to ask after..."

"Days at the beach," he volunteered.

"Exactly!"

He shrugged. "But you can have a pass. Ask any dumb questions."

She faltered. "My questions aren't dumb."

He cocked his head with a laugh. "I'm glad one of us knows. I have a lot of questions, about a lot of things, and hell if I know which ones are dumb."

Ashley waved hello to someone over Phillip's shoulder, and he turned to see Devlin.

His cousin greeted him with a back slap. "What is it? Three days in a row?"

"Something like that." Phillip glanced at Ashley. "I understand you two know each other?"

"No introductions are needed," Devlin offered. "It's lovely to see you."

"Likewise."

Devlin turned to Phillip. "Ashley singlehandedly saved the holiday dinner we hosted for our boat owners."

"It would've been a nonevent, except that two gentlemen overindulged and got into something like..." Ashley deferred to Devlin.

"A food fight."

"Wait, what?" Phillip asked. "I didn't hear about that."

"You did, but the brilliant Miss Cartwright spun the whole problem into a charity event."

"I love charities," she downplayed and blushed.

Phillip's jaw dropped. "The lobster-throwing thing?"

Devlin laughed. "You got it. Boatworks's charity lobster throw started as drunken shenanigans between two surly grumps. Merry Christmas and happy holidays to all."

"There was a lot of talk to make it an annual event," Ashley added.

Devlin nodded. "The woman can work magic."

"Would you like to join us?" Phillip asked.

His cousin shook his head. "I told Hannah I'd grab take-out—"

Something had caught Devlin's eye, and after a small head tilt, Phillip repositioned in his chair and followed his line of sight. *Graham.*

"Huh." Phillip rubbed his jaw. His uncle alone at the Vault wasn't interesting, but the company at his table would raise more than a few eyebrows.

Ashley caught on to their unspoken questions and picked up her purse. "Excuse me. I need to make a phone call."

"She's perceptive," Devlin said after she excused herself.

"She's a lot of things," Phillip added under his breath.

Devlin laid a hand on the chair next to him, lifting his chin.

Phillip nodded. "Take it."

"Do you know those men?" Devlin asked in a way that let Phillip know he already had the answer.

He stole another quick glance at Graham's corner table, tucked away but not out of sight. "Real estate developers, I think."

"Yeah, from a big-time consulting firm out of Boston."

"Huh." Graham hadn't mentioned entertaining out-of-town guests. "Blueprints?"

"Surveys, maybe. I don't know. I can't get a good angle without being obvious."

"We could say hello," Phillip suggested.

Devlin nearly laughed. "It's been a long time since we've been scolded for interrupting."

They both chuckled. When a business ran in the family, family time often became business time. They'd learned early not to disturb.

"Did you hear…" Devlin stole another look.

What hadn't Phillip heard? Even when he tried to avoid the gossip, he still heard more than enough. "About the property lines?"

Devlin's brow furrowed. "Think it's true? About the deeds?"

"Trading hands in a poker game?" Phillip chewed the inside of his mouth. "If so…" He whistled low. "There'd be consequences."

"Enough that Mom would be pissed."

Phillip couldn't imagine how Aunt Claire would handle that, especially if it had happened years ago and was just coming out now. "And Nana would definitely know about a drunken poker game," Phillip added. "But why would they meet in public?"

"If it's true, maybe that's why they're meeting in public."

"I don't get it," Phillip said.

"A public meeting would put out the word. Big-shot

agents and lawyers have hit the street. A none-too-subtle way of showing the world that we're always ready to protect our name."

Phillip worked that possibility over. The family was far more likely to handle private business outside of the courts. A lack of transcripts and records had served them well over the years. That was the whisky business.

"Certainly would send a message." Devlin shifted. "They're wrapping up."

The men in expensive suits with briefcases and portfolios left ahead of Uncle Graham, who paused and eyed both Phillip and Devlin. He held their gazes for a long moment, then left without saying hello.

"He saw us," Phillip grumbled.

"You think?"

"Not even a quick goodbye."

Devlin rubbed the back of his neck. "Something's going on."

Phillip nodded. "Now we sound like everyone else."

Ashley returned, clutching her large purse and tentatively holding her phone. "Is everything okay?"

"Of course," Devlin said as Phillip said, "Sure."

She retook her seat, and Devlin stood up.

"Don't leave on my account," Ashley said.

"I'm not. I was only here to grab a to-go order." He threw his thumb over his shoulder. "But we should meet up later. Hannah wants to visit a festival somewhere off I-95, about an hour away. We'd love for you both to join us."

Heat crawled up Phillip's neck. What was Devlin doing?

"Thank you, but I can't," Ashley answered.

He could've thanked her for handling Devlin's unsubtle matchmaking invitation, but he wouldn't have minded the time together. A festival wasn't on his top-ten list of things to do. But hanging with Ashley when she couldn't cling to the charities or car show was something he could get behind.

"Next time." Devlin offered his goodbyes and left shortly with his order.

A quiet lull fell between them, and Phillip sensed that Ashley wished she'd said yes. She perked up, forced a smile into place, and produced her notebook. "This is what we have from The Laumet Society silent auction." She turned the page. "This is the cash value insurance will provide for damaged goods."

He pursed his lips, reviewing the damaged items. "They're going to give you a check?"

"I think so." Her gaze stayed on the notebook. "Replacement costs for most everything."

"That's great—Wait, what's the problem?" he asked, reading her face.

"Nothing," she said too quickly.

"Ashley?"

"Their agent mentioned..." She pulled her gaze up and winced. "They'll likely try to recoup their loss."

His forehead pinched. "What—Oh, they want me to pay."

Ashley groaned. "I know you're already doing so much, and I—"

"Hang on."

"I told them about the car show, and the—"

"Ashley, listen."

"I'm sorry," she whispered.

"Don't be. I screwed up."

"You're already doing so much."

"*I screwed up.* They're doing what's right. Get it from me, get it from my insurance, get it from somewhere. That's what insurance companies do."

She tapped the page. "Phillip, that's a lot of money."

Ashley was right—that wasn't cheap. But in the grand scheme of things, he might consider it an investment. After all, he'd crashed a golf cart and hadn't killed anyone, and now here they were. "Thanks for looking out for me." He closed his hand over hers. "That's sweet. But I promise—I'm good for it." He winked.

She laughed, her head dropping. "I know."

Phillip rubbed his thumb over her knuckles then eased away. "Just look at it like this."

Ashley looked up. Her watery eyes and an apologetic smile wrapped around his chest.

"What's happening here," he said. "It's all for a good cause."

His double meaning had been obvious. The charity work was obvious. But their back-and-forth, fueled by history and chemistry, would be a good thing as well.

"What else is in that notebook?" He sipped his whisky, understanding her unspoken gratefulness at the subject change.

They reviewed a list of new donors to improve the car show. A few of the names were reaches. Some would be impossible to connect with on short notice. But there was one name that Ashley quickly skipped over—Robert Paget.

Phillip knew him in a three-degrees-of-separation way. Robert had given to the car show before, but Phillip hadn't been the one to ask. They'd never gotten on well. Phillip wasn't everyone's brand of whisky.

Ashley rested her pen against her cheek. "Let's talk about Robert Paget."

He could sense a complication. "That guy. Where to begin?"

"Oh." Her expression clouded. "You know him?"

"In passing. We don't get along."

She tapped the pen against her cheek. "Why?"

Phillip shrugged. "This is a small world, and he's a stiff corporate suit."

"An expensive corporate suit, maybe," she suggested. "It'd be helpful to work with him."

Robert Paget had a history of flashy donations. He loved the attention as much as he loved the tax write-off. "The guy doesn't like me. But to be honest, he doesn't really know me."

She shrugged and drew a line through his name. "You don't like him; he doesn't like you. We can scratch that name off our list."

Phillip straightened, never one to back away from a challenge. "I didn't say it's not worth the ask."

"But it's probably not," she said too quickly.

"Do you know the Pagets?" he asked.

"Sort of. He's friends with my mother."

Phillip made a face. "Enough said."

Her gaze evaded his when she should've at least laughed. "What's on your mind?"

"Nothing."

"It doesn't seem like nothing." He followed her line of sight but found nothing of interest.

"What's back there?" she asked, angling for another change of topic.

"A private game room." A sudden urge to pull her from the crowd ran through him. "Would you like me to show you?"

That had her attention. "Sure."

"On one condition."

She rolled her eyes. "Of course there's always a condition. What is it?"

"We pitch to Paget and ask for a car," he said. "You work your magic. No one says no to you."

"Of course they do—"

"And maybe the guy will act like he likes me."

Her eyes narrowed. "What did you do to him?"

"Nothing. I swear." Phillip crossed his heart. "We're just two different kinds of people."

She hummed as she considered the condition. "If I agree to pitch him?"

Phillip grinned. "You'll get a private tour of the Vault, maybe the distillery, and, fingers crossed, we get one hell of a car."

Her pupils flared, making clear her interest resonated with the private tour more than the car. Phillip leaned forward. "What do you say?"

A soft blush colored her cheeks. "Deal."

What had started as a simple offer of a tour had built into an urge for time alone.

"But we need a plan," she added, too quickly, as though reading his mind.

Phillip saw a flicker of desire flare in her eyes. "A plan for our tour?" The corners of his lips pulled. "Why's that?"

"A plan because," she continued, "without one, we could get distracted and off track. Nothing would get done."

He'd never wanted for a distraction so badly before. His chest tightened, but he pulled back. There was merit to a plan. Hers might be short term—set objectives to wrangle their chemistry then spark a fire that neither would be able to resist—but he would play the long game.

Step one: Show her that golf cart crash was a one-off and rebuild her trust.

He'd grown up since the last time they were together. That didn't mean he didn't have a few tricks up his sleeve. But they were funny, not dangerous or involving live animals. He was well on his way to mastering step one.

Step two: Counteract the vileness her mother had planted in her subconscious.

Ashley couldn't realize how much he knew about Agatha Cartwright. But even knowing what he did, Phillip didn't think he had the full scope. Ashley, however, had developed a something akin to a backbone when it came to her mother. At least that was how it seemed to him. For whatever reason, he was grateful she hadn't taken the helm of her mother's media conglomerate.

Step three: Remind her that they work.

They had sizzle and pop in spades, and damn, it was killing him not to lick her from head to toe. How could she say no to that?

Step four—

"Are you listening to me?" She scowled.

Well, hell. He pursed his lips. Listening was probably important to include with steps one through four, as was telling the truth. Wasn't that all he'd ever wanted from her? "Sorta."

She squinted but sighed and leaned back. "And after that, I'll make a call today and set up the meeting."

"Sounds good." Phillip watched as she jotted in her notebook, somehow fully focused again on the auction details. Her brow knitted as she reread what she'd written, then turned a page, crossing out and circling what looked like bullet point items. "All done?"

Her chin lifted and her lips parted. "For now."

"Come with me." Phillip took her hand. She barely resisted as he pulled, only slowing to grab her purse. The closer they came to privacy, the stronger his urge to rush. Her fingers flexed into his, and he yanked open the door. They stepped into the cool, dark room as the door shut.

Her quick breaths mirrored his. Phillip didn't bother for the light. Their stomachs touched. He backed her to the wall. Their only sounds came as racing breaths. Phillip let her hand go and lifted his arms, caging her to the wall. His heartbeat galloped. Arousal blinded him from reality. This was what she'd run from on the beach. This was what he shouldn't do. But this was everything that he needed.

He wasn't sure if she might kiss or slap him. He would take either because at least that was something—a reaction, an uncoiling, something where Ashley didn't ignore the chaos driving them together.

Her breathlessness gave a quiet whimper, and he couldn't

decipher what she wanted next. Until he knew, he needed to back off.

Phillip swallowed hard. "This is the backroom." His heart punched in his chest, and he couldn't—wouldn't—make a move unless she made her intentions clear.

"Not what I expected on the private tour," she whispered.

That was as clear as mud. "What did you expect?"

"I haven't figured that out yet."

A knot tied in his throat. She needed to do that first. His molars ground, and he knew he needed to back away. She'd drawn the line for now, and he wouldn't take her mouth. "Let me know when you do."

He inched away. She grabbed his waist.

Fire shot through him, and his voice dropped low. "You're killing me." The vibrations rumbled in his throat. "I missed you. Do you know that?"

"Yes," she whispered.

"You left me." He pulled from her hold. "Damn it, Ashley. You walked away. Do you know what that did to me?"

His eyes had adjusted to the dark room, enough that he could read her expression. Emotion stormed in her beautiful eyes. But so did need and arousal, that very basic chemistry and connection that made them fly. But he'd just mapped out a plan, one that would've stopped this from happening, where he'd proven to be responsible and reliable. "Anything else you'd like to see on the tour?"

"I'm not sure," she said.

Answers like that were going to drive him insane. With a deep breath, he jerked the door open. "Set up the Paget meeting. I'll be there." But not right now. It was his turn to run away.

CHAPTER FIFTEEN

THE MEETING WITH Robert Paget had materialized quicker than Phillip had anticipated. He'd had barely enough time to pull himself together before he had to meet Ashley and Robert Paget the next day.

Ashley stood by his side, looking every bit the part of a fund-raiser ready to make her pitch. Her bright dress painted her the picture of King Harbor society life, but it was her high heels that Phillip most appreciated and were hardest to ignore.

"Ready?" he asked.

She nodded, and Phillip drew back the heavy, ornate door knocker and let it fall. The knock seemed to echo cavernously on the other side of the door. "That's a bit pretentious. Who doesn't have a doorbell?"

She elbowed him. "Shhh."

Phillip grinned, glad that she seemed to have forgotten their almost kiss the day before. "I'm just saying. Even a normal door knocker. But that one all but played the drums."

Ashley tried not to laugh. "Be quiet and behave."

"All right." He shoved his hands into his pants pockets, and he shifted his weight, swaying like the wisteria overhead lightly blowing on a breeze.

"How long's it take to answer the door?" he muttered.

"Are you nervous?"

"I don't get nervous." Then he flashed her an impish grin. "Are you?"

"No comment."

Surprised, he gave her arm a reassuring squeeze when the door swept open.

A well-dressed woman with silver hair tied into a bun greeted them. "Good afternoon."

"Hello," Ashley said. "Ashley Cartwright and Phillip Blackthorne for Mr. Paget."

"He's expecting you. Please come in."

They were led into the expansive main hall then shown down another. Given Phillip's upbringing, wealth didn't catch him off guard often. But Robert Paget had always been different, and his home in King Harbor was exactly as he'd imagined—times a thousand. Everything Robert Paget was known for collecting seemed out on permanent display.

The collectibles were legendary and had been detailed in numerous profile pieces. Newspapers from the *New York Times* to the *South Beach Herald* had dedicated countless pages of print to his eclectic collections of rare plants, beautiful art, and historic maps that had guided history. But the collection that had garnered the most attention over the last several decades had been his cars.

Then, with a grand sweeping gesture from the silver-haired woman, the double doors of Mr. Paget's office opened. His office matched his hallways. Collection displays lined the walls. In Phillip's opinion, it tried a bit too hard to be impressive. But he was the one here making the ask, so his assessment didn't mean much at the moment.

"Welcome." Robert Paget rose from an oddly carved desk as they entered his office.

Phillip slid his hand across Ashley's back, eyeing Paget as he stayed across the room.

Ashley stepped from his touch, drawn to one of the many distractions throughout Paget's office. Phillip supposed that was why the man remained by his desk, letting visitors drool over his displays. Phillip let Ashley meander, and he approached Robert for a handshake. The grip was cool and corporate, somewhat surprising given the overelaborate décor, but their exchange bordered on terse.

Ashley approached Robert, and they exchanged a greeting that struck Phillip as personal and friendly.

"I'd heard about this desk," Ashley said, studying the carvings.

Phillip didn't think it deserved the awe that it seemed to inspire in Ashley. The carvings in the wooden structure didn't follow a pattern. Tunnels, bridges, hills, and drops covered the desk without an obvious design. "It's interesting."

"Ms. Cartwright." Mr. Paget produced a small silver ball from his jacket pocket and offered it to Ashley. "How's your mother?"

She took the silver ball, showing it to Phillip as she studied it. "She'd doing well. And your family?"

"The same."

The silver ball was as interesting as their small talk. Phillip wanted to get down to business.

"Drop the ball in the divot at the corner," Robert directed Ashley.

Small talk and a demonstration, but he feigned interest in whatever was about to happen.

Ashley did as told. The heavy ball made a rich sound as it dropped, picking up speed, and spun through the carved maze that was the desk.

Phillip tracked the ball, privately admitting the desk to be awesome as he tried to figure out where the momentum came for the ball to continue its pace.

Somehow, the ball surfaced on the top of the desk by Paget's side.

"That's amazing," Ashley gasped.

Phillip's eyebrows arched. "That was impressive."

"That's art," Paget added.

The trick led them into a more comfortable conversation, though at times their small talk seemed stilted. Then Mr.

Paget leaned back in a high leather chair that resembled a throne more than a piece of executive furniture. "Chitchat aside, you're here for business."

"Business," she agreed, "and charity."

"Not my forte." Mr. Paget hummed then steepled his long fingers together. "I was at the golf charity event that Mr. Blackthorne destroyed."

So much for the meeting moving along in a good direction. "Crashed," Phillip corrected. "The event wasn't destroyed, per se."

Paget cut a harsh, disagreeing glance at Phillip, then softened again as he looked her way. "All right. I don't have much time left. What is it that you need?"

"We were hoping you might be interested in donating one of your cars to a charity car show." Ashley didn't sugarcoat their request. She retrieved the corresponding documents for their pitch. "The Laumet Society and Camp Sunshine—"

"Your nonprofit," Mr. Paget directed to Phillip.

"Yes, sir."

He nodded, and she continued. "Together, we're raising funds for a similar goal. Children. Families."

"And I'm the closest thing you have to the Hope Diamond of cars that you can get."

"Yes," she agreed.

That was a bit grandiose, though Phillip kept that to himself.

Paget's face tensed with his furrowed eyebrows and terse lips. "I'll think about it."

"Thank you," Ashley said.

That was better than the "no" Phillip was certain they would get. No sooner had Paget given them a noncommittal answer than the silver-haired woman arrived to show them out.

After the heavy door shut behind them, Phillip shielded his eyes from the sun. "How'd you think that went?"

Ashley hurried ahead, and he decided that he liked Ashley's ability to banter with the crabby old man as much as he liked how the dress swished as she led the way to his car.

Phillip jogged to catch up. "How do you cover that much ground in those shoes?"

"Practice."

"I bet." Everything about her was practiced to perfection. He opened her door and helped her inside the low-seated Porsche.

Phillip settled into his place behind the wheel and turned the engine over. It was only then that he realized his stomach was about to growl. "Are you hungry?"

"I need to get to work."

That wasn't an answer. "You have to eat." He shifted into gear and eased away from the Paget house.

Ashley laughed quietly then rattled off her to-do list as though she were committing it to memory when he knew the opposite was true. Everything she'd said had already been written down and memorized. Her running commentary of things to do was nothing more than her fearing a quiet, nonwork moment between them.

After the private tour gone wrong, he couldn't blame her.

After driving through the center of town, he slowed at an open parking spot.

"What are you doing?" she asked.

"I'm parking. We need to eat."

Ashley sputtered excuses about how she didn't have time and wasn't hungry then glanced out the window. "You won't fit."

It was like she'd issued a challenge to the parallel-parking gods. "Ha." Phillip checked his mirrors then grinned. "I've heard that before."

"Phillip!" Ashley squeaked, her cheeks flushing pink.

He winked, shifted into reverse, and eased the Porsche back. Smoothly, he straightened the wheel then pulled forward. Once in the tight space, he deadpanned, "Get your head out of the gutter."

"It's not!"

Phillip couldn't hide his laughter. "Well, I'll be damned. Look at you with the dirty thoughts."

"You're incorrigible."

"Whatever you want to call it, beautiful."

Ashley pointed her finger at him, repeating herself, "Incorrigible." She pushed from the car, announcing she would pick the restaurant.

"Whatever you say." Phillip couldn't shake away the grin that Brock had called dopey, and he didn't care. So long as she didn't run away.

CHAPTER SIXTEEN

"THAT'S IT?" MARY Beth pursed her lips in disbelief, ignoring the melting ice cream cone in her hand. "You're telling me that nothing happened."

Ashley nodded, twisting her cone, and wondered why nothing happening made her feel hollow. "Nothing at all. Just a little joking before lunch, and then he was a perfect gentleman."

They focused on their melting ice cream cones before Mary Beth asked, "Are you happy about that?"

"Good question." She leaned her elbows on the bistro table and immediately regretted it. The tables at Dairy Fairy were the stickiest in town. Ashley would know—she considered herself an expert of King Harbor ice cream shops. She grabbed a napkin and wiped her elbows. "Do you think Dairy Fairy would be interested in having a stand at the car show?"

"Who doesn't like ice cream?" Mary Beth licked her ice cream cone. "It'd be a hit."

Ashley pulled out her notebook to jot down the ice cream idea.

"Put your notebook away," Mary Beth demanded. "This is a no-work zone."

"Just give me a second." Ashley twirled the cone, trying to keep up with the melting ice cream drips while writing.

"No work at the Dairy Fairy."

"Fine." Ashley tucked the notebook into her purse then

quickly caught a delicious drip before it slid into the paper wrapper.

"Is that…" Mary Beth shrunk, almost as though her ice cream cone were a shield.

Ashley turned toward her best friend's dread, and her stomach dropped. "Oh God." Her mother and her ex were walking side by side down the sidewalk.

"What are they doing here?" Mary Beth whispered.

"*I don't know.*" Ashley wanted to ditch the cone and run. Not only because her mother and ex would see the ice cream as needlessly messy and a waste of time, but because she didn't want to know why they were in King Harbor together.

What kind of mother wouldn't let her daughter know she was coming into town? With her ex…

Both Mother and Sean were the type of people who saw ice cream as pointless and relationships as nothing more than facades for business mergers and acquisitions.

"Should we go inside?" Mary Beth asked.

They didn't have enough time. Ashley numbly shook her head. "It's too late. They'll see us."

"Then what do we do?"

Her queasy stomach somersaulted as she ran through a list of possible options and discarded each. "We do the only thing we can. We say hello."

Mary Beth groaned but didn't offer any other suggestions. She sat in the chair, wearing an expression similar to a deer caught in headlights, and silently pleaded for Ashley to change her mind and run.

As her mother and her ex closed the distance, Ashley conjured as many calming thoughts as she could. She studied the way the two carried themselves with such cool collection that it seemed impossible they were walking down a street in King Harbor's summer heat.

"Here goes nothing." Ashley pushed the heavy wrought iron bistro chair back and stood. Her ice cream cone trembled, and her fingers tightened their grip on it as she willed herself to remain calm. What she wouldn't have given to momentarily make her ice cream disappear. It was such a silly thought, but the urgency with which she felt it summed up everything about her relationship with both her mother and her ex-boyfriend.

"Mother," she called out, immediately catching the pair's attention. "Sean."

He smiled with recognition. There was hardly a difference between his phony corporate grin and an authentic one.

"Ashley Catherine," her mother greeted with a darting glance at the ice cream cone. "What a surprise." Her closed-lipped smile was nothing more than a polite formality as she and Sean came to a stop by the bistro table. "And Mary Beth."

Mary Beth rose to meet the conversation. She did a good job of hiding her true feelings, but Ashley could see her tension grow as she pushed her heavy chair back. "Mrs. Cartwright, what a pleasant surprise."

"Likewise, dear."

Ashley mentally snorted and wondered if Mary Beth's two first names were the only reason why her mother didn't seek out the middle name to include. Ashley was never simply Ashley.

She gestured with her hand and offered the two free seats to her mother and Sean. "I didn't know you were coming to town."

"Yet here we are." Her mother declined the offer to join them with a flicker of a faux smile and a small step away.

"I'm sorry we can't join you," Sean added. "We're meeting my father for lunch at Montgomery's."

"It seems you've had a meeting with Mr. Paget," her mother said.

"How did you know that?" A trickle of ice cream dripped onto her fingers. Ashley tried to ignore it.

"I mentioned it," Sean volunteered.

How much did they chat? "Oh. Well, yes, the meeting was to discuss an upcoming charity event."

"You should have called me," Sean said pleasantly. "We all could have met at Montgomery's."

Ashley feigned disappointment. "That would've been great. But it was just a quick meeting—"

"Still, I would have loved to help."

Ashley shifted, uncomfortable with his attention, or rather his intentions. "I didn't realize that you were involved with your father's cars."

"I'm not." At that, Sean grinned toward her mother. "But until we can catch up again, your mother has kept me looped in."

Her stomach tumbled. *Looped in on what? Golfpocalypse?* That didn't seem as interesting of a topic for them to share, and her mother didn't do gossip unless it served a purpose. There was nothing for Sean to keep up on except, as her mother hoped, maintaining the amicable possibility of something with Ashley in the future.

Never, ever would there be anything between Sean and her. Sean didn't care that she had ended things between them. There wasn't bitterness. There wasn't even emotion. They had little in common, as they'd quickly learned during their rather dull courtship. He was generically handsome in a squeaky-clean way. Even the way he kept his hair clipped and combed bored her.

But oh my, they had a tremendously overlapping social Rolodex. Her mother would say, "What more does love need?"

Certainly not the same ZIP code. Sean lived in New York City. But between him and Ashley, they were six degrees of separation away from the who's who of Wall Street and American media. Her mother had already mentally married them off before the first date was in the books.

"Ashley, do you need a napkin?" Sean offered.

"No." Impulsively, and suddenly irritated, she licked the melted ice cream off of her fingers and cone. "But thank you."

A quick glance revealed that Mother was almost dying. Ashley wondered what her mother's fans would say if they saw the real Mrs. Cartwright; the one who never tended to her garden but instructed her staff to fertilize, weed, and trim; the woman who had long ago given up hours in the kitchen. The kitchen was now only journeyed to for photo shoots and taste tests of dishes suggested by her editorial team.

Her mother's snooty Goody Two-shoes act wouldn't go over well, Ashley mused. Or maybe fans would forgive her. Maybe they would suggest that she had *earned* the opportunity to step back. After all, Agatha Cartwright could do no wrong.

"How is Phillip Blackthorne?" Mother asked with barely disguised disgust.

The problem poofed to perfect clarity before Ashley's eyes. Mother excelled at playing three-dimensional social chess, and Ashley could visualize the strings she had pulled behind the scene with both Robert and Sean Paget. "Phillip's fine. I'll tell him you said hello."

"No need," Mother added shortly.

"His nonprofit has stepped up to help with—"

"And rightly so after the mess he caused," Mother said.

"It was an accident." Ashley defended Phillip against the same words she'd lobbed at him earlier.

Sean checked his Patek Philippe watch. "We should get going. But it was nice to see you again."

"We'll talk later," Mother said as way of saying goodbye. "Try answering your phone when I call."

The pair left as smoothly as they'd rolled in. Ashley dropped to the heavy metal chair like a wet sandbag.

"Wow," Mary Beth muttered as she dropped into her chair as well and quickly lapped her melted ice cream off of the cone. "If I had known that would happen, I would have told you to stop sending her to voice mail."

Ashley shook her head as she cleaned up the side of her cone. A series of scenarios tumbled through her thoughts. "Her arrival has nothing to do with my avoiding her phone calls."

Two lines creased above Mary Beth's nose. "Then what?" She groaned. "Don't tell me it's because of…"

Of course it was. "She's here because of Phillip."

Mary Beth groaned again. "I was afraid you would say that."

"I'm going to eat my ice cream and pretend that didn't just happen." There had to be a ratio of happiness to ice cream. The more ice cream she ate, the happier she was.

"That'll definitely work." Mary Beth snorted then licked her lips.

"Maybe my mother needs an ice cream cone to lighten her mood up."

"Ha. She needs more than a sweet treat to do that."

"True." Even if Mother enjoyed the lemon Prosecco lavender sorbet that had made the front cover of her magazine this month, that wouldn't clarify the situation.

Ice cream and happiness weren't a solution, and Phillip wasn't the problem. Her mother's controlling obsession was, and Ashley didn't know how to make anything change.

"What are you thinking?" Mary Beth crunched her cone. "You look like things need to be deciphered."

Deciphered was always the right word when it came to Ashley's mother. Until today. "No need to decipher. She's an open book this time."

Mary Beth arched her strawberry-blonde eyebrow. "Then what has your wheels turning?"

"What she's doing with Robert Paget, Sean Paget, and Phillip." Ashley took a messy bite of her ice cream cone. "She's strengthening alliances and inserting herself into the situation."

"Because that's a perfectly normal and sane thing to do."

They ate what remained of their ice cream cones in silence until the treats were gone. Then Mary Beth asked, "Were you ever serious with Sean?"

Ashley shook her head, unable to recall a single instance in which she considered the possibility of a future with him. "Not even a little bit."

"Did he know that?"

Ashley shrugged. "He didn't really care."

Mary Beth's mouth formed a silent O, then she added, "I'm not surprised actually."

Ashley sighed. "Neither was I."

Mary Beth wiped her mouth with a napkin. "Guys like Sean marry for connections and then dilly wherever their fun takes them."

Ashley balled up her napkin and agreed. "Yes, but when did we ever use the word *dilly*?"

Mary Beth laughed. "We use it whenever there's a chance that a man has his underwear starched and pressed."

"Ha!" Ashley choked. "He probably does, though we'll never know."

Mary Beth gathered her purse as Ashley collected their trash.

"Are you ready?" Mary Beth turned away, not waiting for her answer.

"Ms. Cartwright."

Ashley let her eyes sink shut at the familiar sound of Bitsy calling from behind them.

"Oh boy," Mary Beth muttered. "We didn't make it away unscathed."

They both waved, and Ashley mumbled her agreement. "It's going to be one of those days."

"I can't handle this heat." Bitsy waved hello and beckoned, ambling by their table with every assumption that Ashley and Mary Beth would follow. They did.

Both girls pushed in their heavy bistro chairs, which scratched against the sidewalk. Ashley hurried to throw their napkins away and catch up before Bitsy started in on whatever she wanted them to hear.

The older woman had a way about her. Ashley was sure that in her heyday, Bitsy was the life of the party. She still was in her own way. It wouldn't be hard to imagine Bitsy dancing on a barstool in a minidress. But that may have been a decade or two or three ago. A minidress and heels were a far cry from the orthopedic-yet-stylish sandals and the designer linen beachwear Bitsy was wearing today. Ashley knew that outfit was one of many in the woman's expensive wardrobe rotation.

"We're like puppies," Ashley mumbled under her breath, knowing Mary Beth could hear. "We come when called."

"Maybe we'll earn a treat." Mary Beth cracked herself up.

Bitsy turned around sharply, and Ashley thought they were busted.

"Lemonades?" Bitsy announced more than asked before urging them up the two steps next to her and propping open the split double doors to The Aspen.

Air-conditioning washed over Ashley. At once, she became aware of how sticky her skin felt from relaxing in the sun and how frizzy her hair had probably become from the beach wind. At least she still wore a cute dress.

The Aspen was an upscale restaurant that leaned toward an older, expensive crowd that enjoyed their lunches. Several of Ashley's clients could be found holding court over drinks with crushed ice in crystal tumblers at this restaurant on a regular basis.

The host greeted Bitsy like she was a queen then escorted her with a familiar-yet-formal manner.

"Do you think Bitsy knows who's eating at Montgomery's right now?" Mary Beth asked as they trailed the woman.

Absolutely, Ashley thought as she waved to an old family friend. "I'd say that is exactly why Bitsy has us here now. She loves when tongues wag."

Mary Beth walked to one side of the table and grinned. Ashley took the seat across from Bitsy, to Mary Beth's left, and mentally noted the very public table. Bitsy acknowledged a few people in the room with a smile or a flick of her wrist then ordered drinks for the three of them without menus or discussion. Watermelon and lemon juice, sweetened with sugarcane, over crushed ice.

That might not have been what Ashley would have ordered, but it sounded amazing.

Bitsy leaned back in her chair. "Now that it's just us girls, let's talk turkey."

CHAPTER SEVENTEEN

A COOL BEACH breeze blew over the Blackthorne estate's deck as the screen of Phillip's cell phone illuminated at a quarter past seven in the morning. He wasn't a morning person but liked to finish the majority of his day's work by eight a.m., when others first started their day.

He glanced at the screen on his phone and saw Robert Paget's name displayed. His morning calm was shattered by catapulted nerves. This was the phone call he and Ashley had been waiting for. Phillip was certain there were no more questions to ask and no more points to negotiate. Yes or no, he would know the answer.

Phillip answered. "Good morning, Mr. Paget."

"Did I wake you?" Mr. Paget asked.

"No, sir. I'm actually starting to wrap up my workday."

"Ha." Mr. Paget chuckled. "I never took you for an early bird."

Phillip eased back in the teak wood chair overlooking the beach, wondering what had changed the man's surly demeanor. But he let it go. With the morning sun risen and casting a beautiful glow of orange and red across the water, he didn't have time or interest in fueling their drama. The lapping water at the foot of a beautiful sunrise always gave Phillip a sense of calm. "I try to start each day by four thirty."

"Likewise. Did you know that about your father?"

Phillip's breath caught, but he quickly recovered. "No." But the words sounded more like a question than an answer.

Mr. Paget sighed. "What a good man, your father."

A boulder lodged in his throat. He licked his bottom lip and breathed through the unexpected turn in conversation. "Did you know him?"

"Not well, but well enough. I knew that he was someone that could be caught at the office before anyone else so that he could always be the first one home."

The boulder in his throat seared like it had become molten hot. Phillip closed his eyes and pinched the bridge of his nose. So many years had passed, and he still hurt. The guilt still weighed heavily on his shoulders. But it was Mr. Paget's mention of his father being the first one home that caused Phillip to drift decades back. He recalled how his father had never joined them for breakfast. He also remembered that Dad was home every afternoon that he wasn't traveling, ready to play ball after school or push him about homework. Phillip had been too young to note or care why his father was home or wasn't.

Actually, his father being home was a point of contention with Phillip when so many of his friends had parents who'd left them in the charge of nannies and staff. But his father had been there, preaching about hard work and homework, explaining that school was Phillip's job and that struggles would lead him to success.

Every lecture had crawled under his skin, but suddenly, the picture became clear. His father had wanted to spend time with them at home. He'd worked early. He'd come home early. His guiding, pushing, teaching, encouraging...

The molten-lava boulder in Phillip's throat thickened, and he ran his bare feet along the decking underneath the table, clearing his throat. "I guess that's something that we all have in common," he finally said.

"It's not a bad habit to have," Mr. Paget said, seemingly missing the struggle that Phillip was having with the conversation. "Now, about a car to donate."

Phillip took a slow breath. He wasn't one to cross his fingers for luck or pray for an answer that best suited his needs, but a thick ribbon of hope tied into his chest. "Yes, sir."

"I'll let you have one. What do you say about a '55 Mercedes-Benz 300CL Gullwing?"

Whoa! Shock jumped through Phillip's muscles. At the same time, his subconscious warned him not to get excited just yet. He felt a condition lingering close by. "That's fantastic news. Ashley will be thrilled. Thank you, sir."

"But…"

Ah, Phillip's subconscious was right. There was a condition, and those were never good.

"I'd like my son, Sean, to take part in the process."

Phillip waited for another condition, but it didn't come. That was it? Working with Sean Paget? "Of course. That won't be a problem."

"He's not interested in cars, but his interest in philanthropic efforts has grown. This would be a great opportunity for him to see the executive side of charity."

Whatever that means. "Sure," Phillip agreed.

"You can have the car if you loop him into meetings, contractor negotiations, and whatnot. I'd guess there's more nuance with charity negotiation than with the way corporations do business."

Phillip disagreed, but he wasn't going to share that he thought not all corporations were vicious and cutthroat. The Blackthorne empire had grown the whisky business to what it was today because of family, partnership, and trust. They didn't rely on fine print and unscrupulous terms and conditions. They had a strong brand, good values, and excellent recipes. No one could compete with their process. But it wouldn't do any good to explain that to Mr. Paget. "It's a different world."

"I'd say you two should hit the links to meet, but…" Mr. Paget chuckled.

Phillip managed to muster something close to laughter. "I'll get a hold of him, and we'll work something out."

They ended the call, and Phillip jumped out of his chair, pumping a fist in the air. Then he closed his laptop for the day and grabbed his phone, heading for the beach. As soon as his feet hit the cool morning sand, he called Ashley. She answered on the third ring with a sweet, sleepy "good morning."

"We got a car from Paget," he said. "Not just any car. A '55 Mercedes-Benz 300CL Gullwing."

"Wait." Her slumberous softness vanished. "Are you serious? Is that the one with the doors that open from the roof?"

"You better believe it, beautiful."

"Oh my! I was sure that he wouldn't agree. Never mind. I just can't believe it!"

"We should celebrate," he suggested.

"Yes!"

Though he didn't have any ideas on how to celebrate yet. "How about—"

"Ice cream!"

He chuckled. "I was thinking about something a little more substantial."

"Do you like ice cream?" she demanded with an odd worry to her tone.

"Yeah. Who doesn't like—"

"In a cup or cone?"

He laughed again. "I didn't realize this was such serious business."

"Then why aren't you answering, Phillip?"

"Can I say both?"

"No."

"All right, all right. Um—"

"Tell me," she interrupted, "what would you do if your ice cream cone started to melt?"

Has she lost her mind? "Ashley—"

"What's the answer?"

"You're serious," he said, laughing.

"As a heart attack, Phillip."

"If I had to choose between a world of only ice cream cones or ice cream cups, then I opt for a cone, not giving it a chance to melt. Though I do like it when it starts to melt in a cup, especially with toppings." What the hell were they talking about? He didn't care. He loved her laugh. "I'm going to laugh later when you blame this conversation on a sleeping pill."

"You're laughing now," she corrected. "You get three options to handle melting ice cream on a cone, and you can only pick one. A, you lick it. B, you wipe the sides of your ice cream cone with a napkin. Or C, you throw it away."

"B or C, obviously."

She gasped. "What?"

"Ashley, calm down. I was kidding." He let the cool sand wiggle between his toes. "Are you feeling okay?"

Phillip heard what sounded like Ashley throwing herself back into a heap of pillows. "Yeah, sorry," she muttered. "My mother got in my head about something."

"Say no more." Agatha Cartwright was a ninja of manipulation. Somehow, he wasn't surprised that her mother had warped something as simple as melting ice cream. "Are we still on for ice cream?"

"Yes. Do you want me to meet you at the Dairy Fairy?"

A better idea struck him like lightning to a tree, and he grinned. "I'll pick you up."

"Okay, sure."

"How about at nine o'clock?"

She grumble-laughed. "I don't know if I can wait that long to celebrate with ice cream."

"I meant nine in the morning."

"That's pretty early," she said with a smile dancing in her voice.

He grinned. "I'll pick you up in a little less than two hours."

"Phillip," she asked warily. "What are you up to?"

"Absolutely nothing." He said goodbye and disconnected the call then wondered how hard it would be to get an unscheduled helicopter on such short notice.

CHAPTER EIGHTEEN

N OW THAT PHILLIP had an idea of how to celebrate, he couldn't see anything else. Frustratingly though, that included figuring out how to find a helicopter and pilot on such short notice. Waves crashed over his bare feet as he turned toward the house. Light shown from Uncle Graham's wing of the estate. He would know if a helicopter was available or where to come up with one if not.

Phillip jogged toward the compound as he mapped out the day.

Showing up with a helicopter would surprise Ashley. She wasn't necessarily a fan of surprises, but this one was too good to pass up. For the briefest moment, he hesitated, recalling the last time he thought something was a bad idea that was worth it. *Goats in a classroom.* That had been disastrous. That had also been stupid. That wasn't a helicopter.

There was nothing stupid about this idea, and he bounded up the stairs from the beach, barely slowing as he let himself in.

After dusting sand from his feet, Phillip headed toward where the lights were on. He raced down the hall and into the quiet, cool room with bookshelf-lined walls. The library still managed to bring the airy King Harbor beach brilliance into the stately room filled with tombs of beautiful hardcover books.

Uncle Graham glanced up from his paper and coffee as Phillip stopped and tried not to pace. "I have a question for you."

Uncle Graham chuckled. "I assumed you need something, considering the way you ran in here." He folded his paper as Phillip took a seat. "What has you running down the halls?"

A girl. Phillip grinned before he thought better of saying that. "Can I use a helicopter for the day?"

Uncle Graham tipped his head back and laughed. "How many kids ask to borrow the family helicopter on a given day?"

"I'm serious, Uncle Graham," Phillip said, uncertain how much detail he should give.

"Where are you taking it?" His uncle teased as if Phillip had asked to borrow the keys to the family station wagon. "And who will you be with? What time will you be home?"

"Uncle Graham…"

His uncle winked. "How about this, then? Business or pleasure?"

That was a good question. They were celebrating a business deal. Obviously business. He was celebrating with Ashley. Obviously not business. "Both."

"I see." Uncle Graham took a lazy sip of coffee. "When?"

"In about an hour."

His uncle's quiet chuckle became a belly laugh. "Now I'm curious. What are you up to?"

"I promise, I won't get into any trouble." Phillip crossed his heart. No stunts. No adrenaline. Nothing other than ice cream and a beautiful woman. Though the combination made his heart race. Ashley wasn't a punch of adrenaline, but she was absolutely something he couldn't get enough of.

"I didn't ask about trouble," Uncle Graham pointed out.

Impatience vibrated under Phillip's skin. Uncle Graham had every right to ask about his plans just like Phillip had every right to request use of the helicopter. If he needed to find a new idea, he could, but he didn't want to let this one go.

"I've heard you've been spending time with Ashley."

Phillip straightened, surprised.

"That smile is answer enough." Uncle Graham sighed, amused. "Yes, you can use the helicopter. Call the Enterprise office, and they will coordinate the quick request."

"Thank you." Phillip bounded up.

"I'm not done yet." Uncle Graham gestured toward the chair.

Phillip dropped into the chair, apparently not dismissed yet.

"I prefer to hear what's going on from you," Uncle Graham said. "Not from your brothers or cousins."

"There's nothing—"

"Don't feed me a line, Phillip."

"With Ashley?"

"Unless there's another woman who has your attention and needs a helicopter."

Phillip drew in a contemplative breath and let it out slowly. "It's been years..." Years since she broke his heart, since he let her walk away, since they were too young to know what mattered in life and how to hang on to cherished people. "But somehow, that doesn't seem to matter."

"Do you love her?" Uncle Graham asked with a serious bent to his tone.

Phillip coughed. A blush heated his cheeks, and he had no idea what to say. They didn't talk about relationships. Uncle Graham had given all the boys *the talk* and had kept them in gear—not only to stay safe but to protect the family name. They, however, did not do heart-to-hearts. "I, um..." he stuttered. "We dated in college."

"I know that." Uncle Graham lifted an eyebrow. "Are you going to tell me something that I don't know?"

Phillip squirmed under Graham's steadfast scrutiny. "She hates me."

His uncle did as close to an eye roll as his manners would

allow. "I can see that."

Phillip grinned and scooted to the end of his seat. "I don't know what to say, but I have to go."

His uncle nodded, releasing Phillip.

Rushing from the library didn't slow Phillip's hammering heart or cool the heat in his cheeks. *Do I love her?* Impossible.

They didn't know each other anymore. Too much time had passed. His interest in her was stereotypical and cliché, driven by history, jealousy, and a possessiveness he couldn't let go. Ashley was gorgeous. Her beauty flew off the charts just like her success and intelligence.

Those surface-level qualities would always be a draw, but he knew their connection went far beyond attraction and explosive chemistry. But none of that meant love.

Flustered, Phillip questioned what Uncle Graham knew about love. He was the one who couldn't keep it after thirty-seven years of marriage. He was alone, unwilling to admit that he wanted to be with Aunt Claire, wondering where she was or who she was with. Uncle Graham was too stubborn a man to fight for what he needed: Claire.

Phillip's stomach dropped. The similarities between Graham and Claire and him and Ashley shined bright, glaringly obvious.

What if Graham waited as along as Phillip had before seeing Ashley again? Why waste that much time?

Phillip went to his suite and called Blackthorne Enterprises. After a quick conversation and an assurance that Phillip's helicopter request would be scheduled, he called an old friend and asked for a favor before finalizing his plans.

Phillip dropped onto the corner of his bed. The question of Graham and Claire continued to weigh heavy in his thoughts. If Graham waited years to find Claire, would they still have their love? Or had their love already gone before Claire left?

Hell, dissecting their relationship made him feel as uncomfortable as trying to discover the big family secret. Still, Phillip wondered if the answers to the future lay in their past.

He dropped back onto the mattress and watched the overhead fan spin lazy circles. The answer was easy, simple. Love didn't leave because of time or distance. It might fade. It might be forgotten. But love would always exist, even if gone, ready to be forgiven and unburied.

Or maybe he'd lost his mind. Phillip pinched the bridge of his nose, uncertain about the wave of realizations making his blood run hot and cold. But given his logic, he'd never stopped loving Ashley.

The more he tried to discredit his rambling thoughts as a fallacy, the more he became certain she'd always held a special place in his heart. Worse—or maybe it was a good thing—he believed now that he'd always loved her. Even to this day.

CHAPTER NINETEEN

FIVE MINUTES UNTIL nine a.m., and Ashley couldn't wait a second longer. She said goodbye to Mary Beth, who was already at her desk with numbers on her screen and industrial-looking headphones over her ears.

Ashley shut the door, doing little to insulate Mary Beth from Mother and her people, who'd taken up residence in the beach house guest rooms. Some people packed their own luggage. Her mother did not. She had people to pack, then she brought those same people to unpack—a personal assistant, some kind of manager, and a personal chef. Ashley hated them, and they never left.

The irony wasn't lost on her that Mother seemed completely helpless while manning an empire of do-it-yourself, entertain, and decor.

Even if Mother's people weren't milling over coffee in the dining room, Ashley itched to escape. She couldn't stop thinking about what Phillip had up his sleeve.

Without disturbing the *people*, Ashley crept out her front door, checking her phone. He would arrive at any minute.

The door reopened as she settled on a porch chair. Mother stepped out. "What are you doing out here?"

Hiding. "Not much." She wondered where her mother had been as she'd made the rounds, but she didn't ask, instead fidgeting with her leather thong sandal. Her leg bounced. Mother brought a sudden burst of nervous energy.

She scrutinized her outfit. The gauzy white top paired

with the simple navy skirt was a step over casual. Ashley had tried on a dozen looks, choosing one with a decidedly business-casual air. The soft, feminine fabrics flowed over her, making her feel pretty. It was the perfect outfit for... a celebratory ice cream excursion? She didn't know.

"Would you like to come in?" Mother asked.

Ashley pressed her sandals to the front porch. "I'm waiting for Phillip."

"Hmm."

"He's picking me up."

Mother scoffed. "The boy calls, and you just run out the door and wait. I recall him lacking in the manners department, but I didn't realize you—"

"Actually, Mother, he texted."

Her mother cringed. "Of course he did."

Womp, womp, womp. They twisted and looked at the blue sky as a helicopter emblazoned with the barrel-and-thistle logo hovered. A Blackthorne helicopter lowered in the front yard.

Mother gasped. "Oh my word." They were close enough to feel the displaced air shift across their skin, lifting their hair.

The rotors cut, and a door opened. Phillip jumped out and waved.

Ashley slapped her hanging jaw shut then whispered, "My ride's here."

Mother had nothing to say as Ashley numbly waved back. Phillip jogged up the porch stairs and greeted Mother without missing a beat.

Manners *and* a helicopter... Ashley managed to keep that to herself as he shook her mother's hand and offered genuine small talk. She walked a tightrope of not gloating or succumbing to shock of the helicopter surprise.

Phillip broke from the polite conversation and turned. "Are you ready to celebrate?"

"Celebrate?" Mother asked, curiosity pinching the corners of her eyes.

Ashley had no intention of answering as Phillip took her arm, making her heart skip a beat. "I'm ready."

He pulled her to his side, smelling mouthwateringly shower fresh. They closed in on the helicopter, and the door opened. He eased his hand to her lower back, leaning his mouth close. "Surprise."

Phillip helped her in and closed the door. The rotors sounded as the pilot greeted them with a hello. The overhead whine dulled to an overhead thunder, matching her racing heart.

Ashley took her seat and had to catch her breath. She couldn't imagine being more surprised. He grinned.

"Proud of yourself, aren't you?"

He handed her a headset. "Hell yeah."

"Good." She beamed. "You should be. This is amazing."

Phillip adjusted her headphones and her mic. She brushed her hand over his, struggling for words to adequately convey the moment. She'd ridden in helicopters before, but this one left her gobsmacked. The seats were soft leather, emblazoned with the barrel and thistle. The polished wood gleamed, and the shades on the windows were pulled high, allowing for panoramic sightseeing.

"Here we go," Phillip said as the helicopter lifted, swaying slightly as it gained height.

"We'll be there in about an hour," the pilot said.

Her eyes widened, and she twisted to Phillip. "Where are we going?"

"For ice cream."

"I know, but—"

He directed her toward the window. They journeyed over the shore, following King Harbor's beaches.

"This is absolutely amazing," she whispered.

A life-is-good grin hitched on his face, and an urge to snuggle with him tightened in her chest. She wanted to be close. Her skin tingled, and she prayed that his mouth would brush against her forehead and linger. Ashley wanted nothing more than to curl into his arms, to just be. But even if they weren't buckled in, after pulling from him more than once, she wasn't sure of making that move.

Phillip rubbed her arm, and she listened to him extrapolate on King Harbor's history and the slow-changing topography. She soaked in every detail. He'd done all of this for her.

★ ★ ★

AFTER MORE THAN an hour had passed, Phillip could sense that they would soon arrive at their final destination. Disappointment flooded him as the helicopter descended. He'd talked endlessly until Ashley snuggled against him, and then he'd simply breathed her in. Now they would be forced to separate, and he squeezed her close one last time.

Phillip hadn't fully appreciated what winning her back would mean. When he did have her back, he would never want to lose her again. When they were together before, he'd relished the way she could comfort his racing mind, how she'd balanced his search for reckless fun with her sensible, pragmatic style.

Thinking back on their short time together, he saw the importance of connection, of family.

Spending time with her had clearly gone beyond work and righting an old wound. *Why the hell did I ever let this woman leave without a fight?*

Youth wasn't a good excuse. Maybe he was just dumb… or scared.

Hell, he was still scared. He'd let no one become that close to him for fear that they would be another person to lose. She had left. Not in the same way as his parents, but he worried she could always leave again.

The pilot interrupted his thoughts, announcing it was safe

to disembark.

"Where to now?" Ashley stayed close by his side as they exited the helicopter and followed along a path.

He pulled her under his arm, directing them from the private airstrip to where a waiting car should be. "Time for ice cream."

She beamed as he guided her around a corner lined with high hedges. A dark SUV became visible, waiting at the curb of the private airstrip.

"Did I ever tell you I wasn't the most patient person?" Ashley grabbed his elbow and dragged him toward the SUV. Her laughter rang light and carefree, matching the way her bright eyes danced.

The chauffeur secured them in the back seat, and they sat close, their legs brushing together. Phillip angled against the door, and Ashley peered out the window. Her honeysuckle-scented loose hair dangled over her face as she searched for clues.

They drove for only a few minutes before she gasped quietly. "Oh my..." Then Ashley rolled her window down. "Are you serious?"

The larger-than-life sign for Bliss ice cream matched the over-the-top brand with the funky flavors and cult following.

Ashley twisted to face him. "You brought me to Bliss?"

He chuckled and shrugged. "I guess so."

Wordlessly, she shook her head then clasped his cheeks in her palms. The quick, personal touch made his blood burn as his gaze shifted toward the front gates that the SUV turned into.

"This is the nicest thing that anyone has ever done for me." Her fingers drifted softly over his cheeks until the tips lingered along his jawline before falling away.

"I'm glad you're surprised."

"Surprise is an understatement."

They slowed at the front of a colorful corporate entrance,

and the driver stepped out.

They were alone, only for a few seconds, as the driver took his time walking to the back door. But for now, it was just them, sitting together. Her mouth hovered close, his to take. They'd been in this position more than once in the days before, and each time he thought he would kiss her, she pulled away. He needed her to want his mouth like he did hers, unable to turn away.

The door opened. The bright sun and warm summer flooded the back seat, and Ashley jerked away. But Phillip remained still. If he'd kissed her, would she have pulled back like that? He didn't know.

Ashley fumbled for her purse. Her chin ducked, hiding her face and expression under a thick curtain of silky hair before she held her bag in her lap like a shield. "Are you ready?"

Her words were too perky, too rushed. Her smile was too broad and begged for him to ignore the previous moment.

Good thing he hadn't kissed her yet. But he would. He waited an extra second before answering, making sure she knew he saw through her walls, then said, "I'm ready, but I'll wait until you are too."

CHAPTER TWENTY

ASHLEY HAD NEVER been terrified of a kiss. She had a list of reasons to keep Phillip at arm's reach. But now it was the devastating possibility of an unexpected future that kept her away. She couldn't let them be hurt like she'd done before. Still, she didn't stop Phillip when he took her hand.

The morning sun warmed them as they ascended the front stairs of Bliss, and they fell into another world. The sugar-scented air greeted them. The brightly colored reception area reminded her of the brilliant ice cream packaging. Senses buzzed with the anticipation of their day. "This place is…"

Phillip rested his hand on the small of her back. "It's nuts."

She had been searching for a more eloquent word, but his description fit. "Nuts works."

"We're glad you think so."

They turned toward the voice behind them. A woman about their age, who wore jeans and a loose cotton Bliss T-shirt greeted them. "It's nice to see you again, Phillip."

He took her outstretched hand, and they shook. "Like-wise."

"I know you're busy, and I always said that when you had a good reason, you would make time for a private tour." The woman turned to Ashley as Phillip made introductions. Her name was Miranda, and she clasped Ashley's hand with both of hers for a handshake. "It's nice to meet Phillip's good reason."

Ashley blushed. "Oh, well, we're here for work. We're celebrating."

"Work or not, Phillip has never asked for a tour." Miranda walked across the open waiting room and pointed to accolades framed on the walls. One in particular caught Ashley's attention, and she closed the distance to see an article from *People* magazine. On it, Miranda and Phillip held a large check made out to the name of his nonprofit. A very substantial figure was the focal point of the image. "I lost my parents when I was young, too," Miranda said. "I'm a big believer in the work that Phillip does."

He shifted, uncomfortably, and politely interrupted. "Ashley knows me well enough."

True, but not really. They'd talked about business and car show details, but not much about his nonprofit. "I didn't know that you had friends in high places at Bliss."

The slightest hint of a blush warmed his cheeks. "Now you know."

"This one plays it close to the vest," Miranda added, probably sensing Ashley's curiosity and Phillip's modesty. "Let's go for a walk. I'll show you where the magic happens."

They left the reception area, and Ashley was unprepared for the kaleidoscope of colors that covered the hallways. Bright, colorful metallics led to a rainbow of watercolors and then a bedazzled corridor. Monkey bars lined the ceilings, beanbag chairs held court in the corners. Ashley stopped more than once to read brain teasers emblazoned on the walls. They even passed two Bliss employees playing an oversized game of tic-tac-toe as though it were just another day in the Bliss corporate headquarters.

"Our company philosophy believes that creativity begets creativity," Miranda added, noting how Ashley slowed down to take in their game.

"I can tell, and obviously it works well for you."

The sugary air was now distinctly lighter and fruitier.

They stopped at a lemon-colored door, and Miranda escorted them into a stark-white laboratory. Everything—the ceilings, floors, cabinets, and workspaces—was a gleaming, glossy, lacquered white. There wasn't a sign of life or any telltale signs of what happened in the room. There were no pens, pencils, papers, or computers, and not the slightest hint of ice cream.

Phillip turned slowly. "This is not what I expected."

"It never is." Miranda's impish grin warned them that the day would be full of surprises. "Take a seat."

They pulled white metal stools from under an expansive table that was surprisingly cool to the touch. At Miranda's command, the center of the table separated, and a chill kissed the air. A small platform, only slightly smaller than the large workspace they first sat at, arose from within the table without a sound. There were several white bowls filled with brightly colored fruit. Some looked juicy and ripe, while others appeared frozen or dusted with sugar.

"This is the testing ground for our new sorbet concoctions," Miranda explained as she produced white aprons from a discreet closet and then set a platter in front of them holding stacks of small bowls and spoons. A moment later, she added serving utensils. "We start with the freshest, ripest fruit and then imagine the best combinations. That's what you'll do right now. Close your eyes and let your taste buds call the shots."

Ashley wasn't sure about closing her eyes. The display was breathtaking, and the fruit deserved attention. Her mother's magazine could snap pictures of the display, as is, and it would be magazine ready.

"You want us to try these?" Phillip asked as he took a spoon. "I think we can manage."

"I do. But there's one more thing." Miranda crossed the room and returned with a tray of small glass pitchers. Each had a label etched into the clear glass: agave, sugar water, honeysuckle nectar, and so on. "Some of these are more acidic. Some can be overpowering, while others you won't be able to get enough of."

Miranda took a small bowl and ladled mangoes and bananas together. She expertly crushed them with what looked like a petite potato masher, added a splash of agave, stirred once more, then took a bite. Her eyes sank shut on a quiet *mmm*. After a long moment, she smiled. "If this isn't on the shelves within a year, I might throw a fit." She winked. "No Fool's Gold. That's what I want to call it, but I haven't convinced the board of the name."

Ashley took a small spoon and dipped it into the bowl that Miranda offered. "I think it's a fantastic name."

"I'm glad you think so." Miranda beamed. "Now dig in, and I will be back in a few for our next part of the adventure."

Miranda left, and the room became slightly awkward. Both Ashley and Phillip hesitated. "I don't know where to begin." The amount of possible combinations overwhelmed Ashley. "I feel like I'm going to mess up."

Her confession was all it took to break Phillip's unease. "Nah." He took a bowl and piled it with raspberries. Then he took a second bowl and added strawberries. "Our taste buds are calling the shots. There's no right way to do this."

She wasn't convinced. "There might be. Not everything makes it onto the shelves." Ashley carefully took her bowl and added blueberries then poured sweet cream over the top of them. "What if I add too little, or too much?"

His fingers flicked her knuckles, splashing more sweet cream than she had intended into the bowl of blueberries.

"Hey!" Ashley placed the pitcher on the table and studied what was clearly more sweet cream than she had intended to pour. "Mess with your own creation."

He snickered. "I bet it will taste just as good."

"But it wasn't what I had planned." Ashley took a tiny potato masher, stirring and squishing the mixture together. "It doesn't look very pretty."

"The looks don't matter, you know?" Phillip took his spoon and mashed the fruit in his bowls.

"I think we're supposed to use different utensils for each bowl." Ashley gestured to the large display of spoons and implements. Carefully, she continued stirring until she deemed the consistency perfect for a sample. Then she dabbed the end of a fresh spoon into it for a taste test.

"Oh," she groaned over the small bite. "This is fantastic." She took another spoonful, this time confidently eager for more. The mixture didn't look like much, but as Phillip had mentioned, appearance wasn't what mattered, at least not in this room. Taste was everything. Her combination was a winner.

He took a large spoonful from her meticulously crafted bowl.

"Hey—"

With the spoon still in his mouth, Phillip nodded and groaned his approval. "That's good."

He came back for a second sample, and she tapped her spoon on his. "Don't mess with my bowl."

Her attempts to keep her bowl safe failed. He snagged another dripping spoonful. "Thank you."

"I had no choice." She laughed. "What are you doing?"

He mixed the heaping spoonful from her bowl into his bowl of sugary strawberries and swallowed the messy mixture, groaning his approval. "It's better this way. Try it."

"No."

He tried to steal another spoonful from her, and Ashley shielded her blueberry bowl. "Your strawberries are going to mess up my blueberries."

Undeterred, he took another scoop from her bowl, mixed it with his, and effectively stopped her argument when he pushed the spoon into her mouth.

"Oh…" The strawberry-blueberry combination made her see stars.

"Good, huh?" He took the spoon back. "And to think, ten seconds ago, you were terrified that my strawberries would ruin your blueberries."

She rolled her eyes. "Don't gloat."

Then he added, "You should trust me more. This is the part that you always get wrong."

Ashley stiffened. "Yes, because I'm always concocting new fruit-and-sugar recipes."

He grinned and laid his spoon down. "No. But you are certain there's only one perfect way to do something, and any deviation is second best."

"I do not!"

The yellow door opened, and Miranda walked in. "Are you ready to move on?"

"You do too," he whispered against her ear before pushing up from the stool. "Absolutely. Where are we off to next?" Phillip held his hand toward Ashley to help her off the stool.

He was wrong! Just because she saw things one way didn't mean she didn't think another way could coexist. Stiffly, Ashley moved alongside Phillip as they followed Miranda and she explained the history of the sherbet room.

"Don't be mad at me," he teased.

She wasn't mad. She was annoyed, and she elbowed him to make that point clear. "I'm not."

But annoyance wasn't her problem either. Her stomach turned as she realized that her inflexible refusal to stray from a decision, a thought process instilled by her mother, was more prevalent than she'd even realized.

CHAPTER TWENTY-ONE

T HEY MOVED INTO a warmer hallway. The scent of hazelnut and vanilla now hung in the air as Phillip's old friend led them down a darkening corridor. Gone were the bright colors transposed against stark-white walls. Now they were surrounded by wall textures and soft lighting. Deep mauves and warm, rich chocolates replaced the glossy lacquered finishes.

Ashley didn't seem to notice the gradual transition. She stiffly walked next to him with an expression as rigid as her posture.

"You're really not mad at me?" He risked her anger as he slid his hand across her back.

Before Ashley could answer, Miranda's cell phone rang. She mouthed an apology as she took the call, walking away.

"No." Ashley crossed her arms and turned to face him. "I'm not mad at you. I'm mad at me."

His eyebrow cocked. "Don't do that. Come on, it's our day of fun." Her expression didn't change, and guilt needled him. He wouldn't have teased her if he'd realized she would take him so seriously. That had always been the problem between them, though. Worried that he'd misstepped like he had in the past, Phillip offered a conciliatory grin. "I promise I was joking."

Ashley sighed. "Don't mind me. You just hit a nerve."

He was good at that. Phillip rested his hands on her shoulders, playfully giving her a small shake. "I was teasing. It was all in good fun."

"Either way, you were right."

He laughed. "I don't hear that often, but I don't know that I'll take it if it comes with a frown and—"

Her shoulders stiffened as her face drew tight. "I pride myself on not being my mother."

"Oh, shit, no." He went up as though to block her words. "I wasn't comparing you to your mother. Hell, I wouldn't do that to my worst enemy."

Her smile broke, but she dryly said, "Ha ha."

"I'm serious, Ashley. That woman, I mean your mother, is a shark-toothed people eater. No offense."

"I can't take offense at the truth," she offered quietly.

Phillip's dislike of her mother knew no bounds. There had been times that he thought he couldn't dislike her any more. Then conversations like this happened, and he learned that there were many more levels of dislike to go. "Ashley, you are nothing like your mother."

She shrugged. "Maybe, maybe not. But she was a major influence in my life before..." Ashley's eyes clouded. "At least until she wasn't."

Before what? Phillip had no idea what she was talking about, but he wouldn't blame anyone for babbling incoherently when it came to Agatha Cartwright.

He wondered if there'd been a distinct pivot point that changed her mother's influence, but he wouldn't ask and let it drop, more concerned about Agatha Cartwright thoughts marring their celebratory day.

Miranda reappeared with perfect timing. "I'm sorry about that. Are you ready to taste again?"

"Absolutely," he said, welcoming her interruption. A few strides later, they entered a room that made his stomach growl for more than a few spoonfuls.

Miranda walked them through a similar process, but this time with dozens of chocolates, from the milkiest milk chocolate to a coffee-bean-infused dark, bitter chocolate. Some chocolate was salted, while others were spiced. There were even chocolates that had been mixed with mind-blowing reductions, like those made from bacon and balsamic.

And that was only the chocolate. They had similar containers with vanilla, hazelnut, peanut butter, and more. The choices and combinations seemed endless.

This time when Miranda left, they dove in. Playing with the chocolates served as enough of a distraction that Ashley loosened up again. The more she relaxed, the more he did too.

They tasted what they made, then offered and fed their own creations to one another. This time, they enjoyed the heavenly desserts but equally enjoyed their time together.

When the door opened again, Miranda appeared. A slice of disappointment rested in Phillip's chest. He didn't want their time goofing around to end.

"Now, are you ready to put it all together?" Miranda asked in an upbeat fashion.

"Is it ice cream time?" Ashley whispered with awe and reverence.

"Let's see what we can find." Miranda beckoned them from the chocolate room.

Phillip rested his hand at the small of Ashley's back, guiding her to follow Miranda and enjoying the way she leaned into him. "Ice cream time. Let's celebrate."

She eased under his arm and looked up. "I think we've been celebrating for a while now."

CHAPTER TWENTY-TWO

THEIR TIME AT Bliss had been nothing short of delicious. With a sugar buzz and her guard down, Ashley let herself go. She forgot about her mother, the past, how she should control her feelings for Phillip, and simply stayed in the moment. She hadn't known how hard that would be at first, but then she embraced the newfound freedom.

"Do you need to head home?" Phillip took her hand as the front doors of Bliss closed behind them.

The sun shone high overhead. It was a beautiful day, but it couldn't compete with the magical time they'd just had. She didn't want their day to end. "No."

His eyes danced, and Phillip gave her hand a squeeze. "I have something I want to show you." Their SUV pulled up as if it had known the exact moment of their departure. "Give me a second."

He let go of her hand and met their driver before he'd opened their back door. Their conversation was quick, but when Phillip turned around, eagerness lit his face.

"You look excited," she said and let him shepherd her into the back seat.

He settled beside her and closed the door. "I am."

"Another secret?"

He grinned. "We'll be there before you know it."

"You haven't let me down so far." She didn't move from the middle seat.

He draped his arm over her shoulder. "I don't intend to

start now."

Ashley closed her eyes. The scent of sugar clung to their clothes. She relaxed into him. His chin rested on top of her head. Her heart skipped a beat.

The driver took his seat, and they rolled away from the curb. Ashley wasn't tired, but she couldn't ignore the lull that pulled at her eyes. She let them remain shut and soaked in the way he held her to his chest.

"We're here." His lips tickled against her ear.

She blinked, surprised to have drifted asleep, then glanced out the window as the SUV's smooth drive rumbled. A thick forest of trees lined their route. "Where?"

They slowly rounded a wooded turn. She read a rustic sign. *Camp Sunshine.* Her jaw fell. "This is your place."

"Since we were so close, I thought we could stop by."

She couldn't explain why this seemed like more than an inconsequential visit. "Thank you for bringing me here."

"Truth is, I've never brought anyone here before." He shifted and stared out the window.

Ashley knew that wasn't true. Athletes and celebrities had made their rounds through the camp, but yet she knew what he meant. Family and friends. "Why?"

He shrugged. "I've kept my distance from Blackthorne Enterprises." He snorted. "And they're probably grateful."

"That didn't answer my question," she said quietly.

The SUV stopped, and the driver stepped out. Again, they had a moment of privacy when she wanted time to pause.

"They wouldn't understand."

The door opened. Their seclusion disappeared, but her tingle of awareness stayed. She was special. He believed she would understand. What, she didn't know. Ashley took his hand as she stepped from the vehicle, ready for him to explain.

Laughter and joy danced through the forest. She couldn't see children playing, but they weren't far away. Phillip led her up a gravel path to a cabin. A wood sign that read *Camp Office* hung over a screen door.

"After you," he said, opening the door.

Ashley stepped into a quintessential camp office. From the painted floor with a glowing sunrise to the pine shiplap walls covered with children's art, she couldn't imagine a camp welcome better than this. Friendliness emanated from the exposed rafters. Joy hung in the form of children's crafts. There was no place for grief. Phillip's camp shined a child's reprieve.

The screen door slapped shut, and an older man with a bright grin stepped from a back room.

"Isaiah." Phillip greeted the man with a back-slapping hug.

"What are you doing here?" Isaiah shook his head, surprised, and turned to Ashley. "Hello."

"Isaiah Scott," Phillip offered. "Ashley Cartwright."

Isaiah took her hand, shaking it with a smile large enough to make her beam. "It's lovely to meet you." He turned to Phillip. "Like I said, what are you doing here?"

They laughed. Isaiah's delight was contagious. Phillip added, "I was in the neighborhood."

"Is that so?" He turned to Ashley. "With company like this, I can see how a short drive might end up here."

Ashley blushed. "We went for ice cream."

Isaiah's eyebrows lifted. "I'm sure Miranda will fill me in."

"I'm sure," Phillip said.

"What did you have in mind for your agenda?"

Phillip took her hand. "Nothing much. I'll give her a quick tour."

Isaiah winked. "Take your time."

Embarrassed, Phillip chuckled. "First, we'll swing by the chow hall. What was for lunch today?"

"Corn dogs, green beans, and slaw."

"We showed up on a good day."

"Phshh." Isaiah shook his head. "Every day's a good day,

son."

"Especially when it's corn dog day."

With that, they said goodbye and walked out the screen door. It smacked behind them.

Ashley wasn't wearing anything close to hiking clothes, but she kept up with Phillip when he veered from the gravel path to one worn through the woods. The tree canopies shaded them, and nature's tune mixed with the ever-present sound of kids.

"Here we go," he said as they stepped over a small log that blocked their path then into a clearing.

The chow hall had the same wood sign over the front door. She hadn't imagined what his camp would be like, but this seemed like a storybook ideal. They entered through another screen door, and it made that same slap when it shut. Rows of empty rustic picnic tables lined the large room. Overhead fans circulated the air.

"We came too late to sit with everybody." He guided them toward the far end of the room.

"I can picture you eating with a bunch of kids," she said.

He laughed. "Versus what? Eating alone?"

"How often do you come up here?"

Phillip pushed through a swinging door, and Ashley followed. "Enough that I know corn dog day is one of the best."

"I dare you to name a day my lunches aren't the best."

Ashley spun as Phillip turned, lifting hands overhead, then took the stack of plates in the other woman's arms. "You know I love anything you make."

"He says once he sees me," she tittered.

Phillip set the plates in a cabinet then gave her a kiss on the cheek. "This mama bear is queen of the kitchen and ruler of the roost."

She waved her hand. "Does this one know how to hand out a compliment?"

Ashley held out her hand. "Ashley Cartwright."

"Amelia Scott."

She noted the same last name. "Nice to meet you."

"The pleasure's all mine." They shook, then Amelia turned to Phillip. "Isaiah said you were coming but neglected to mention your guest."

Phillip shrugged. "I can't control that man any more than you can."

Amelia laughed. "Who said I've ever tried?"

"He's her husband," Phillip volunteered.

"Of fifty-three years." She pretended to count on her fingers. "Lord, that can't be possible." Her head shook. "No matter. Make yourself at home. You know where the leftovers are." Amelia walked away, muttering how fifty-three years of marriage was impossible given that she couldn't have been more than forty.

Ashley took everything in then added on a sigh, "I wish I went to camp."

With plates in hand, Phillip stopped. "What?"

She shrugged. "This is everything I imagine camp should be, and I haven't even seen the kids yet."

"Back up to the part where you've never been to camp."

His scrutiny made her uncomfortable. "I haven't."

"How is that possible?"

"Never worked into Mother's agenda, I guess."

Phillip grumbled on his way to the refrigerator. He plated food with a scowl, shoving each into microwaves that lined the counter.

"What?" she asked.

He shook his head. "Tell me how she—"

"My mother?"

"Yeah, the grande dame of summer lemonades and fancy Popsicles, never sent you to camp. How did someone like that end up with her role?"

Ashley bit her cheeks. "I don't know. A good marketing

plan and—"

"Never mind." Phillip turned to the microwaves. "Forget I asked."

"Are you upset with me?"

He looked at her like she'd lost her mind. "No."

"She used to be normal," Ashley said. "Even if she was always more robot than not. I've seen pictures of her and my father doing normal things. Like picnics." Though she couldn't remember family activities like that. "I've read interviews where she discussed cooking and…" She sighed. "You're right. Never mind." It was exhausting to think about.

Phillip took the plates from the microwave and added coleslaw. She followed him to a picnic table. Before they dug in, she desperately wanted to lighten the mood again. "Tell me your favorite thing here."

"Easy. The rope swing into the lake."

"Oh, that sounds like fun."

"Next time, we'll bring our swimsuits," he said. Then he took a bite of his corn dog.

Next time. She grinned and then devoured her lunch.

CHAPTER TWENTY-THREE

THE LAKE GLIMMERED with activity. Phillip leaned back in his Adirondack chair, admiring the view. Or rather, admiring Ashley. Somewhere between the chow hall and the lake, she'd let herself go, and a lack of beach clothes didn't stop her from playing with the kids.

A group of twelve-year-olds schooled them in volleyball. Phillip blamed the ugly loss on a day filled with eating, but Ashley borrowed a hair tie from one of the girls, playfully demanding a rematch.

He and Ashley lost that game too. Then a game of cornhole. That was all he could take. But she stayed with the kids, playing in the water with the groups that cycled through their day.

Her skirt and shirt were soaked as she tried to catch minnows with younger kids. Never in a million years could he have pictured this. She turned, as though feeling his gaze, and gave him a quick wave.

His chest tightened, and her smile drew him to his feet. Ashley covered her eyes as he made his way to her. Sweat glistened on her forehead. Tendrils of hair had escaped the ponytail. Best of all, she didn't care. He wasn't sure she'd ever looked more beautiful.

A whistle blew. A counselor called for the kids to line up. They ran from the water, but Ashley didn't move. By the time Phillip's feet touched the water, the group was heading out, singing a camp song about s'mores.

"Is everything okay?" she called.

Phillip waded into the lake and stopped in front of her. The water came to his knees, and she tipped her head back as he towered over her.

"This has been the most amazing day ever," she whispered.

He wanted to give her that again and again. "Good." He brushed the loose hair from her face. "You need to know something."

"What?"

"I promised myself I'd slow down, take things slow."

Her eyes widened.

"I haven't kissed you yet, but I'm halfway in love again."

Ashley trembled, and not giving her time to second-guess or run away, he took her cheeks in his hands. Phillip bent close. Her eyelashes fluttered, and he pressed his lips to hers. Her hands clutched his shirt, and she opened her mouth to him.

He savored the fullness of her lips and the greedy way she pulled him closer. He relearned her mouth, every sweeping second heightening their intensity until they clung together. Phillip gathered her in his arms and slowed their frenzy until they swayed together, lips a breath apart.

She nuzzled into his chest, letting him wrap her in a hug.

He couldn't recall this possessive hunger before, and if this high was only halfway to love, he wasn't sure that either of them were prepared for him to claim her.

CHAPTER TWENTY-FOUR

B ETWEEN ICE CREAM and kissing Ashley at camp, Phillip was spent. The afternoon became a blur after they left the lake. Nothing specifically changed between them. He'd already taken to holding her hand. But that kiss didn't leave a lot of room for them to ignore what was rekindling between them.

He would wait to figure out what that would mean. They were exhausted. The helicopter lulled Ashley to sleep beside him, and Phillip thought long and hard about directing the pilot to take them to the estate. *Slow down, don't rush* became the prevailing advice in his head.

The helicopter descended where they'd picked her up almost twelve hours before. He carefully woke her as they landed.

Her groggy ideas refocused. A quiet smile curled on her lips. "Thank you. Today was more than I expected."

He unbuckled them and pulled her close, letting his lips brush over hers. Exhausted or not, their kiss heated to life. It was a good thing that he'd brought her home. If they were alone, he would push her too fast. "I'll walk you to the door."

Her front yard was dark, but several lights were on in Ashley's house. He helped her from the helicopter, taking her arm to the front porch.

"We didn't discuss work today," she whispered, turning into his arms.

"We're not going to start now." He kissed her good night. "But we can over dinner tomorrow?"

She nodded. "Sounds like a plan."

If she only knew how much of his plans he'd hung on tonight. "Good night, beautiful."

★   ★   ★

THE NEXT EVENING felt as though it would never come. Phillip had checked his watch a half-dozen times before leaving to pick Ashley up. After yesterday with a pilot and a driver at the helm and today's anticipation for dinner, Phillip relished the control of driving.

"I love the Bickmore," she said.

The engine purred as he leaned into the gas on the straightway. "It's never a bad decision to dine there."

His cell phone rang through the Bluetooth. The dashboard screen illuminated, and his cousin Ross's name appeared.

Phillip glanced toward Ashley. "Do you mind if I take this? He might have news about the stock car test drive."

"Please."

Phillip accepted the phone call. "I was wondering when I might hear back from you."

"If it's not one thing, it's another." Ross laughed.

"Yeah, guess so." They hadn't talked much since Ross had a heart-stopping wreck. He'd walked away from the flames nearly untouched. "How's Holly?"

"She's great." The smile in his voice carried through the speakers.

Phillip couldn't have imagined his daredevil cousin settling down, but Ross had done so while happily falling in love—even if he'd once promised not to lose his head over Holly. "You sound good, man. I'm happy for you."

Ross chuckled. "There must be something in the whisky."

Phillip snorted. "Must be." Devlin, Jason, and Ross had all fallen hard and fast this summer. "Tell Holly to keep an eye on the mash." As the woman in charge of their Kentucky operations, she would know if the Blackthorne brand had been dosed with a love potion.

"Three out of the seven of us? Less than half. I won't be concerned unless you drop too, Philly."

He would've groaned over the nickname, but instead, heat hit his cheeks unexpectedly. Phillip cleared his throat. "Let it go, Martin."

Ross chuckled.

"Who is Martin?" Ashley asked.

Phillip held up a finger and would explain their Martini & Rossi inspired childhood nicknames later. For now, he was more concerned about the conversation drifting toward relationships. "So, about the donation, all we need is a car and someone to drive the highest bidder around a track."

"That's all you need, huh?" Ross cracked. "It took some time to find room on the calendar since the team won't be in that part of the country any time soon. But there's a small block of time we can do after the Green Mountain 500."

"Really?" Phillip mused. "That's great. Your text led me to think it'd be impossible to work out."

"At the time, it was impossible, but when you pull my sponsors into it, things change."

Phillip slowed for a turn. "What are you talking about?"

"You didn't need to sic the Cartwrights on me."

His eyebrow cocked, and Phillip stole a confused glance at Ashley. "What?"

The Cartwrights were one of many corporate sponsors of Ross's team. Aggravation crawled up the back of his neck.

Ross continued. "Brock mentioned that you were working with Ashley Cartwright."

"I am, and she's in the car."

Ross paused. "Hey, Ashley. How about this for an introduction?"

"Hi," she said quietly.

Phillip couldn't get a read on her reaction to what Ross had said. "What do you mean about the Cartwrights and your sponsorship?" He had the distinct impression that he couldn't see a big part of the picture. "Ross?" He slowed behind a driver, finding himself stuck at the speed limit. "What do the Cartwrights have to do with your schedule opening up?"

"Everything when Agatha Cartwright and Sean Paget issue an ultimatum to our director of corporate sponsorships. Donate time on our schedule, or we lose their sponsorship. I made the schedule work—did you not know this?"

Phillip's blood ran cold. "No," he spat out, glaring at Ashley. In the shadowy sunset light, her skin had taken on a decidedly pale pallor. "I haven't even met with Sean yet."

Ashley jerked toward Phillip. "What?"

But Phillip was more concerned with Agatha Cartwright than an overeager guy stepping onto his turf.

Ross seemed to sense the tension, adding, "However, the details need to be communicated. You have a lap with one of our stock cars to auction off."

Unease turned in Phillip's stomach, but he managed to say, "Thanks. I owe you one." Then he ended the call.

Ashley didn't make a peep, and that alarmed him on several levels. He pulled into the drive at the Bickmore Hotel and left his Porsche before the valet stepped from the curb.

Ashley had opened her door, but Phillip jerked it wide, less concerned with manners and more driven by the unease piling onto his shoulders. "What the hell is going on?"

"Can we talk inside?" She tentatively stood from the passenger's seat and clutched her purse in front of her.

"No. Answer me now."

Ashley pushed her hands in front of her, using the purse as a barrier. Exasperation radiated. "I don't know."

"I'll tell you what I know. Your mother is in town. You didn't mention that, and I only found out when I crossed paths with Her Majesty yesterday on your front porch."

Ashley shifted her gaze, and Phillip took her by the elbow, leading her inside the hotel. His quick pace did little to make her robotic walk hasten by his side. Out of frustration, he stopped and ducked them to the side of the lobby. "Explain. Now."

"I don't know." She shook her head, pressing fingers to her temples. "They arrived a few days ago. I saw them when Mary Beth and I were at Dairy Fairy."

"Them who?" Phillip demanded.

"Mother and Sean."

Phillip's teeth clamped, and his nostrils flared. "Part of my agreement with Robert Paget is to show Sean the ropes, to take him behind the scenes of a nonprofit."

"Three-dimensional chess." Ashley grew paler and looked sick as her eyes shut.

"What does that mean?"

"Nothing," she muttered. "Just that I hate her."

"You say that a lot."

Her angry eyes tore open, and Phillip could see the hurt that glared, though he wasn't sure how much of it he had caused. It didn't matter. This wasn't the time or place to dig into that.

"Never mind." Phillip turned away. He wouldn't be caught dead working on anything in which her mother was involved, and Ashley knew that.

"Wait," Ashley called and pulled on his arm.

He shook her away before noticing more than one set of eyes watching with gossipy interest. He wasn't going to be part of the King Harbor tongue-wagging squad tonight, so he turned them down a hall clad in roaring twenties décor. "Let's go this way."

Ashley kept up with his quick pace, and he tucked them away into a quiet art deco alcove. "You have to explain more than what you've said."

She looked everywhere but at him.

"Ashley," he demanded through clenched teeth.

"All right." Tears colored her voice but didn't brim in her eyes. "What do you want to know?"

"Hell, anything." His temper burned in his chest. Phillip ran his hands into his hair. "What else haven't you told me?"

She swallowed hard. "I haven't told you that Sean Paget is my ex."

CHAPTER TWENTY-FIVE

"Your ex?" THE tendons in Phillip's neck strained as he repeated what she'd said.

Regret made her nauseous. She should've mentioned Sean before the meeting with his father. She'd tried, half-heartedly, but gave up like a big chicken because she didn't want to add more confusion into the mix with Phillip. Clearly, wussing out was a mistake.

Phillip's lips thinned, turning whitish as though he were pinching his mouth shut to avoid an explosion. Then he snapped, "I have to go."

"I didn't know what they were doing," she tried as he stormed away. "I should've said something before we met with Robert."

"You think?" he cracked without slowing.

He was too far ahead of her. Chasing him was fruitless. It was last-resort time. "Wait," she bellowed, causing several people to turn and stare. He turned, well aware of what she was doing. "You can't just leave me here."

"Fine," he relented through sealed teeth and pivoted toward the front of the lobby. "Catch up."

She had to race to do so. They burst outside, both their tempers flaring. His Porsche had only been moved to the side, and Phillip didn't wait for the valet manning the station to retrieve the vehicle. The two men shared an unspoken conversation, and the valet tossed Phillip his key fob. He caught it in one hand, not even slowing for the catch or to say thank you. "I'll get you back tomorrow."

"You always do." The valet nodded to her as she rushed to keep up. "And have a good night, miss." *Customer service over everything.* That must have been the Bickmore's motto.

The Porsche's engine roared as she nervously joined Phillip inside the car and shut her door. Immediately, the tires squealed before she'd even situated herself.

"Buckle up." Phillip cut a sharp turn from the Bickmore's drive.

Ashley tugged on her seat belt. "Do *not* drive like a moron because you're pissed at me."

"I'm not."

"This is what you always do. Do you know that?" she screamed.

His fingers flexed on the steering wheel as a tightness pulled across his face.

"Do you know that?" she yelled again.

He braked hard and pulled over. The seat belt cut into her shoulder.

"Do I know I do what?" he growled. The engine roared as though he'd taken off again.

Her heart raced. Anger climbed into her throat. "This." She threw her hand across the interior of the car. "You create distractions. You speed up when you should slow down. You—"

"You have no idea—"

She grasped his forearm and shook him, screaming as loud as she could. When the screech stopped, her throat ached. His eyes were wide, shocked, but she had his undivided attention, even if her voice was gone.

Ashley swallowed, and it hurt. Her fingers loosened on his arm, but she wouldn't let go. "I didn't know anything about Mother and Sean that was worth a conversation," she whispered. "Much less an argument."

He faced out his window and stared blindly ahead. Fury

radiated in his profile, and still she didn't let go.

"I need you to believe me."

"I believed you once before." Hurt replaced his anger. "Why should I believe you now?"

The past had come back to haunt her, and she could offer nothing that she hadn't said before. "I don't know."

CHAPTER TWENTY-SIX

T HE DRIVE TO Ashley's beach house was a quiet one. The short distance seemed to take hours to navigate while simultaneously ending before Phillip had come up with a single thing to say. Ashley preoccupied herself with her phone as it dinged with texts and emails.

Her home looked the same as it had the night before, cloaked in darkness but with several windows illuminated. He parked, torn between the urge to help her out of the sports car and the wish that she would disappear.

Her hand rested on the door lever. "Not that this is what you want to hear, but we have a lunch meeting tomorrow with Sean. Whether you want to go or not, I'll text you the details. Don't decide right now." Then she opened her door, got out, and melted into the darkness.

He waited until a slice of light from the front door illuminated and swallowed her into the big home.

Like hell would he meet with Sean Paget. Phillip shifted the Porsche into gear and crawled from her house. He stayed in first gear, willing himself to push the sports car until the motor offered a high-performance escape, but a hollowness in his gut made the effort too exhausting.

Calling Ross or Brock should have been first on Phillip's to-do list. But thinking about the car show or expectations made the crushing weight of their fight heavier.

Phillip drove aimlessly until he pulled into Harbor Park. It was closed to the public at dark, but he didn't care and exited his car as pointlessly as he had driven there.

Ashley had said that he sped up when he should have slowed down. Hell, he couldn't walk any slower if he tried. Phillip dropped onto a bench that lined the running path. He leaned back. The sea of stars overhead trumped any view at home in DC, where city lights dulled the night's carpet of stars.

But even the King Harbor sky didn't come close to how the stars shined at Camp Sunshine. He'd promised her they would visit again, and his heart hurt that maybe they wouldn't. Bringing her to his camp hadn't been his intention. The trip to Bliss had been more than enough. But he couldn't stop himself from sharing his special retreat.

At least he hadn't told her that was where he'd disappeared to after they broke up. He'd sat in the same Adirondack chair when the idea of his camp and nonprofit had surfaced in his mind.

He hadn't recalled that night in so long, when he'd been lost and decided he would help kids like him from feeling this lonely pain.

The Ferrari 330 GT drifted to mind. His thoughts were on a miserable roll. Phillip dropped his head, hating to lose that car. Would it matter if he could just keep the memory? Even now he could feel the sleek metal frame glide under his palms the morning his dad had brought him into the garage.

Dad smiled proudly. "It's yours."

Phillip's heart leaped. "Really? No way! You're going to let me drive it?" That was the most important question his young brain could manage.

Dad's laughter rumbled. "In a few years." Then he leaned close and whispered, "Or maybe sooner if your mom says it's okay."

Phillip jumped and punched the air with his fists. "She will. I'm sure she will," he nearly shouted, wanting to run to his mom and ask right then. But Phillip stayed put and watched his dad, understanding that this was a moment to share between them.

Dad eased into the passenger seat. His look said a lecture was imminent, but Phillip didn't care, as long as he would get it while sitting in the driver's seat.

"Get in, Son."

Phillip climbed in and rested his hands on the steering wheel. His feet didn't reach the pedals, but they would one day. He beamed at his father, resting his hand on the gearshift, ready for any conversation.

"I gave this to you earlier than I intended," Dad said.

Phillip listened with a small twinge of apprehension. Dad wouldn't tease him then take it away. But he might use it as leverage for him to take school more seriously, maybe life too.

"It needs some work." Dad clapped his hand on top of Phillip's. "And I'd like to do it together."

That was the talk? His apprehension morphed into excitement. His father was a serious man, never thinking Phillip was just a kid. But what if Phillip was wrong? Dad wanted an older kid, the kind of kid he could work on cars with. That had to be it. "I'll do whatever it takes."

The back of Phillip's throat burned. He recalled the conversation, even the most minute details—the smell of the garage, the expanse of his dad's car collection, the family collection of cars, and the cool air that was held at the exact temperature for optimum storage.

But he'd screwed up. He'd been himself, and his dad had never understood that part of him. They'd worked on the Ferrari, but Phillip was still a silly kid, struggling to focus at school. Dad called it giving his parents *grief*. Well, the tables turned on that one.

Phillip ruefully scoffed at himself. Dad had sent him to that wilderness camp with strict rules and regimens. Phillip had known why, even if nobody had said the reasons out loud.

He couldn't be the son that his dad had wanted him to be.

Tears pricked his eyes. He remembered the day when he was called to the camp office. Of course he had managed to get himself into trouble, he had thought. Maybe he simply didn't fit in there either and had to go somewhere else. Then Uncle Graham and Aunt Claire walked in. Their faces were drawn, and their footsteps were heavy on the worn pine floors.

When he saw his aunt and uncle there, fear grabbed him by the throat. The words were a jumble. *There has been an accident. It's time to go home.*

Through the grief and the tears, Phillip sought to find a reason for his parents' death, wanting to wager with God to change the past and erase the accident.

That had been impossible because he had been the reason. His parents died because of him.

Heavy, guilty tears slid down his cheeks, and Phillip mindlessly wiped them away, trying to recall the truths he had learned over the years. The airplane crash hadn't been his fault. The gages were to blame. He wasn't.

But instead of the words he had trained himself to focus on when guilt attacked, he heard Ashley's voice instead. "*This is what you always do.*"

She was right.

Just like Brock and Jason. They never said it, but they blamed him for their parents' deaths too.

There was no point in pursuing Ashley. History had proven he would only screw it up in the end.

CHAPTER TWENTY-SEVEN

To: Phillip Blackthorne
From: Ashley Catherine Cartwright
Subject: Outstanding Car Show Before the Sean Paget Meeting

Ashley stared blankly at the email and blinking cursor on her laptop screen. Unable to articulate her thoughts, Ashley minimized the email message and opened up a browser, deciding to do what she had never let herself do before— google Phillip Blackthorne.

The results were quick and expansive. She scrolled beyond the gossip pieces to the first few pages of the nonprofit sites and news hits. Then she went back to the website for the Camp Sunshine link.

A sliding header of kids smiled as they hung off trees, splashed in the familiar lake, and climbed rocks. Every smile matched happy, carefree eyes. She assumed each child was an orphan, many without the means to go to camp. But in these pictures, they were kids enjoying life. Not lost, grieving souls.

Had she ever seen Phillip as carefree as when they were there? What about her? She'd let herself go. No rules. No consequences. And look what that had gotten her. *Hurt.* But not before they'd kissed. She took a deep breath then clicked through the website.

The About Us page featured the Scotts. Their smiles and love showed more than the accompanying text would explain about their positions. Ashley scrolled again and stopped at a picture of Phillip then read the mission statement.

Mission: To provide a safe environment for children and teens that have lost their parents or caregivers unexpectedly, while giving them the tools for self-care, without the burden of financial worries.

Ashley's eyes filled with tears. She scrolled and read and scrolled and read, finally deciding that Phillip was never too far behind the scenes. He flew under the radar, but his influence reached all parts of the nonprofit. She saw his dedication and talent, doing much more than raising funds. Phillip used his access and influence to bring celebrities, athletes, performers, and more to the camp to aid in the acceptance of mental health and therapy. He made self-care cool. But how much of that had he taken to heart for himself?

CHAPTER TWENTY-EIGHT

A SHLEY DIDN'T EXPECT the hostess at Montgomery's to say her guests had already arrived. *Guests.* Her heart hammered. She hadn't been able to get a hold of Phillip all morning. If Sean brought her mother to the meeting, she would scream. Her hands trembled as she followed the hostess, and Ashley clutched her bag to her chest when they turned toward a more secluded section of the restaurant.

Phillip. Her heart leaped—even as her aggravation multiplied.

Both men stood when she reached the table. She eyed Phillip and greeted Sean warmly enough. "I see introductions are out of the way."

They chuckled like old friends, but Ashley saw through both of their acts. How had either of them beaten her to the restaurant? No matter. She took her seat, having no intention of showing either man how uncomfortable this meeting might be.

Sean sat at Ashley's right and yammered on and on about a yachting race. His family, like the Blackthornes, had teams and interests in yacht racing. She had once thought that Sean only enjoyed sports and society events because they were an opportunity to connect, socialize, and network.

Actually, she wasn't sure what he liked as a hobby, other than climbing social and business ladders. Their incompatibility was so obvious that the idea of a romantic moment with him bordered on hysterical.

She could see that incompatibility, but Phillip, who sat on her left, seemed oblivious to their lack of connection.

The waitress came over, interrupting Sean with their drinks. It wasn't lost on Ashley that Phillip had ordered iced tea while Sean had ordered whisky—a non-Blackthorne brand.

She ordered an iced tea as well, and Sean continued to talk about sailing, retelling a story she'd heard before about sailing despite the threat of an impending squall.

Phillip focused his attention on Sean, but his gaze was dark and untrusting.

Her iced tea arrived, and the waitress made a joke about their serious faces and deep discussion. Ashley snort-laughed—they hadn't even approached a contentious topic yet.

Sean cocked his head. "God bless you."

Another snort-laugh almost escaped, but she managed, "Thank you."

Phillip, confused, cast a sideways glance, keenly aware she hadn't sneezed. That only made her need to laugh more. This was so awkward, and she was making it so much worse.

They placed their orders, all three selecting the special. As soon as the waitress left, Ashley was ready to get to work. She produced a notebook from her purse. "I met with the site manager. We've agreed on the parking spaces reserved for special guests—"

"What's that for?" Sean asked.

"For the car show," Phillip snapped, barely moving his lips. "You know, that thing you keep inserting yourself into."

She extracted a map from the portfolio in her purse and hoped Sean took Phillip's growl for a tremor of car show anticipation. Not likely, but a girl could always hope. After unfolding the map, she pointed to the row of parking spaces with enough gusto that both men took a look. "This section of the parking lot will be cordoned off. Cars will line up here.

Hoods up and engines on display." Her fingertip slid over. "Live music will be over here, and the food and beverage stations will be set up here."

Sean studied the layout then shook his head. "I've never been to a car show before."

"Shocking," Phillip said.

"I must've missed that part of my cultural education," Sean added snidely.

Ashley refrained from smacking him and changed the subject. "All right, that's for the daytime events open to the public. It's relatively simple—pay at the gate, and let the raffles and giveaways run all day. It keeps people around and continues to raise more money."

Sean studied the map and asked doubtfully, "This has worked in the past?"

Phillip's nostrils flared. "Yeah, it has."

"Fascinating."

Ashley glared at Sean, willing him to cut the pompous act, but the tension didn't tone down. Where were their lunches? She might need to pull these two apart before the sea bass special arrived. "The auction would be more familiar to you," she volunteered to Sean. "While its open to the public, bidders have to preregister, and there is a high minimum for the first bid."

"That's what my father donated to?" Sean asked.

"Yes. There is a small number of amazing cars that will be auctioned off. The proceeds will be split via a confidential agreement with the owners donating a portion to charity."

"That sounds like an excellent tax write-off." Sean sipped his whisky, seeming to approve.

"It's for an excellent *cause*," Phillip snapped.

Oh boy. Ashley bit her lip. The tension between the two men spread like a wildfire. She was helpless to do anything but watch them snarl and bicker.

"I understand you dated Ashley," Phillip said.

She choked.

"As did you," Sean volleyed.

"This is a business lunch," she tried.

Sean grinned and laid his hand over hers. "We ended amicably."

She pulled her hand back, still catching how Phillip's jaw twitched.

"Lucky you," he said.

Ashley wanted to shake sense into Phillip. Couldn't he see that Sean wasn't her type? "The raffles are amazing." Her voice trembled, and jittery, she nearly gave herself a paper cut as she fidgeted with the map. "Phillip had an incredible lineup already, and combined with The Laumet Society's additions, I think this will be a huge success."

"Ross Blackthorne offered his team car." Sean leaned his elbows on the table and studied Phillip's reaction.

"We know," Ashley snipped before Phillip had a chance. Unable to hold herself back, Ashley continued. "Is there anything else that we should know?"

"Not that I can think of." Sean grinned. "I'm here to help, but I'm not a miracle worker."

Tension ticked in Phillip's jaw as he sawed his teeth. "I thought you were here to learn."

Sean shrugged. "To-may-to, to-mah-toe."

"I'm so glad we're working together," Ashley interjected, forcing a smile. "As for the raffles—"

"I didn't think we had a choice," Phillip said. "Robert Paget said his son needed to learn a lesson in how to be charitable."

Sean's lips flattened. "And Agatha Cartwright explained The Laumet Society needed a strong hand to help ensure their financial commitments and goals would be met."

That upset Ashley more than it did Phillip. Sean had never noticed or cared about the difficulties she had with her mother. Ashley's cheeks tightened. "Did she? How nice."

Phillip snorted, obviously hearing the snark that Sean missed.

Sean's forehead creased. "Phillip, do you know what I meant to ask you about?"

Her stomach turned, and Ashley didn't know what Sean was about to say, but it would be bad.

"I heard that Claire Blackthorne skipped town," Sean said.

Phillip stiffened. "She didn't *skip town*."

Sean continued. "And there was something about a secret."

"There are no secrets."

Sean tilted his head toward Ashley. "I can't blame the woman for leaving a Blackthorne—"

"Shut your mouth." Phillip's fists clenched.

Ashley gripped his forearm before he could do something they would all regret and tried to tug him away from the table. "Excuse us, please."

Phillip didn't budge.

She gave a firm pull. "Please come with me."

After a worrisome moment, Ashley took a breath when Phillip followed her. She led the way to a back hallway that Montgomery's only used to reach the office and for private events. Then she whirled around toward him. "Do not let that prick get under your skin."

Phillip's anger lingered. "Do you mean your boyfriend?"

"*Ex*-boyfriend," she hissed. "Don't be like that."

"I can be however I feel like being."

"Listen to me!" Her heart slammed in her chest, and she grabbed his arm. "Why can't you see that you're the only significant ex in my life?"

CHAPTER TWENTY-NINE

HIS NOSTRILS FLARED. Greedy possession flooded Phillip, and he couldn't stay away. He gave her no warning, needing her kiss more than he needed to breathe.

Their lips crashed. She wrapped her arms around his neck. His hungry hands covered her body, searching to remap the curves he'd once known so well.

She pulled for more contact. Her mouth tasted of sweet desperation. Carnal need blinded them from anything but one another. Her hands tangled into his hair. Their racing breaths burned together. Every lick and nip brought them higher, closer together, in Montgomery's hallway. Phillip didn't care.

He pressed her to the wall and had never wished so hard to be inside a woman.

She broke from him, gasping. "We can't here."

"The hell we can't," he growled. His erection thickened, and his mind was numb.

"Upstairs." Ashley clung to his biceps and then pushed from the wall. Her fingers grabbed his hand as she glanced over her shoulder. "Quietly."

Excitement pounded in his chest. "Are you serious?"

"Are you coming with me?"

Hell yes he was. He lifted his chin, and she led the way to a dark staircase, then up until she opened a door.

"Do you know where—"

"Shush." She pulled them into a room lit only by the sunlight casting through white curtains. "Never underestimate the secret rooms event planners can find in a pinch."

The large space was relatively empty. He surveyed it, noting stacked chairs that lined one wall. Circular tabletops with their legs folded rested on top of one another in the corner. A random assortment of couches and chairs lined the wall nearest the windows. The room wasn't the least bit romantic. But it was private, and they were alone.

Phillip closed the door and followed her in, meeting her halfway into the room when he grabbed her hips. She melted into his hold, wrapping her arms around his neck when he lifted her up.

"You got me here," he whispered.

"I did." Her legs wrapped around his hips. "Now that you've seen the tour of empty rental rooms, I suppose you're ready to go back downstairs?"

"Ha." His mouth covered hers, and she moaned into the kiss. Just like moments before, they were rabid again. He crossed the room to the row of furniture, stopping at the first couch and easing her down. His heart hammered. He kissed down her neck, sliding his hands along her sides as her hand caressed over the front of his pants.

If he'd stuck to his plan, he would've found a way to romance her before they fell into bed. There would be a fancy hotel room and room service with champagne. Anything she could possibly want.

"Don't stop," she whispered.

He was head over heels in love with her. Knowing that, his plan didn't matter, and he gave them more of what they both craved. Slowly, he slid her skirt up her legs.

"Sexy," he whispered. His hands trailed over the delicate lace of her underwear. "If I had known this was all you wore…" His finger feathered across the front of her panties.

"You're teasing me." Her chest heaved.

"I'm taking everything in."

He explored without touching skin, watching her reactions with every stroke.

Phillip hooked his fingers in the top of the lace and eased it down her thighs. She unbuckled his pants and tugged at the waist of his boxer briefs.

This was makeup sex—from yesterday and from years before. He needed what she offered and removed the condom from his wallet, covered himself, and let her pull him close again. He rubbed against her slickness, kissing her deeply, until he could no longer wait. Their bodies came together, and Phillip pressed into her until he knew nothing but her heat.

They clutched one another. Their wild frenzy tempted him to lose control. But her eyes held his, and he held her, each thrust bringing her closer to climax. There was nothing more that he wanted to feel. Then she cried out, demanding that he never stop.

Phillip rode into her, pulling orgasm after crying, begging orgasm. When his own was ready to hit, he wrapped her to his chest until they both exploded together.

CHAPTER THIRTY

FIRST AND LAST impressions matter more than substance. That beautiful piece of bad advice from her mother had stuck with Ashley like a wine stain on silk. It had been one of her mother's "only inside the house" sayings, designed to give Ashley the winning edge, knowing full well that it would be a disaster if anyone heard her mother's advice outside the home.

It took more than a few sessions to get beyond her therapist's shock when Ashley shared what she knew was an irrational, but ingrained issue—one of many doozies that had nearly given her an existential crisis. Ashley had wanted to be substantial but had to accept that desire before she could own it. That acceptance came after hard work on her therapist's couch.

Now she owned the heck out of it. But it didn't mean that her mother's *advice* didn't rear its ugliness at the worst of moments, like now when she realized that she'd last walked away from Sean to go have sex with Phillip. She was sure the reasons for their departure and delay were as visible as a scarlet letter branded onto her chest.

Phillip's hand glanced off her lower back when they eased into the lunchtime hum of locals and tourists enjoying seafood at Montgomery's. Ashley let him escort her toward their table then stopped abruptly. Their table was empty. Their glasses and napkins remained, along with her bag, safely tucked onto her chair.

Phillip chuckled. "I guess we took longer than we meant."

Did he laugh to alleviate mortification? Because that was what she felt. The red scarlet letter that hung around her shoulders felt like a blinking sign. People knew. They had to. What had she been thinking?

He moved to his seat and lifted a paper bag from his chair. "They packed our lunches to go."

Heat baked her cheeks as Ashley moved her purse and sank into her seat. "I should call him."

Phillip snorted his disagreement as their server reappeared. Ashley couldn't find the words to explain their disappearance.

"Mr. Paget asked me to pass along that he was called to an important business meeting unexpectedly."

If she hadn't known what had just happened, Sean's excuse would have made perfect sense. Phillip set the food aside. "How about that. So were we." He reached for his wallet. "We'd like to take care of the bill if you wouldn't mind."

"It's already been settled. Is there anything else I can get you?"

A rock to crawl under and hide. "No, I'm fine. Thanks for asking."

Phillip pushed back up from his chair, but Ashley didn't think she could stand until their server moved on. She gathered her thoughts while fussing with her purse.

"Come on, Ashley. No one knows."

She side-eyed Phillip but eventually got up and let him lead her through the lunch crowd, tucked under his arm. They stepped into the hot summer afternoon, and they both turned different directions.

Ashley paused. "Where are you going?"

Phillip stepped to her and wrapped his arm around her waist, gesturing down the street with the to-go bag. "To my car. And then to my house."

"I'm this way." She thumbed the other direction down the street.

He ignored her gesture and guided her until they reached his Porsche. He set the to-go bag down and towered over her, close enough to make her throat dry. Phillip cupped her cheeks, studying her eyes as he offered a sly grin.

She wanted to back away but didn't. "Why are you looking at me like that?"

"Because I'm ready to leave, and I'm not sure you're getting in the car without some cajoling."

"I don't think that's a good—"

"It's simple, Ashley. I'm hungry, and you're stubborn. We're both going to eat, and then we can talk." He dipped his mouth close to her ear, and her heart pounded as she imagined his kisses, anticipating a soft touch.

White-hot desire boiled just beneath her skin. She didn't know herself when it came to him. "I'm not stubborn," she said, not convincing either of them.

Phillip dropped a kiss on her forehead then opened his car door and leaned in to start the ignition and blast the AC.

"And I'm not sure I'm ready to talk," she added.

His crooked grin was his best weapon. "Then we won't talk."

A series of hot flashes ignited.

Phillip tilted his head toward the car. "Get in and decide later if we talk or not. Either way, I have to eat. A man needs his energy to keep up with you."

CHAPTER THIRTY-ONE

COOL AIR RUSHED over Ashley, somewhat taking her edge away. She used the opportunity in the passenger's seat to study the Blackthorne estate as Phillip eased up the drive.

She wondered who else might be at the estate and what they might think. Brock would know something had happened between her and Phillip. He'd always been protective over his brother and the Blackthorne family name.

Phillip parked, and she admired his casual demeanor. "Decided what we're doing yet?"

Her eyes bugged. How could he talk about sex so lightly?

"Food," he said, though she thought maybe it was food *first*, then he helped her out of the car and took the bag from Montgomery's.

"Hello?" he called as they walked in. "No one's home, or they're ignoring me."

"Consider me shocked that ever happens," she muttered.

He laughed and led her down the hall and to the lower level. They entered an expansive billiard room with a bar and kitchenette in the far corner. She could only imagine the munchies and snack foods that the cabinets held and the family time that the brothers and cousins had enjoyed together on the couches, watching the large-screen TVs on the walls.

Phillip stopped at a large table and laid their take-out bag on it. "What would you like to drink?"

"Water."

"You got it."

She followed him, then took the plates and utensils that he handed her from a cabinet. Ashley set the table for them and unpacked the bag as Phillip returned with two large tumblers of ice-cold water.

They both sat down, and Phillip dug into his lunch immediately, but she held back and swallowed another round of jitters.

"This is really good," he said, half swallowing a forkful. "It would have been better hot from the kitchen, but given the situation, I like it this way."

A mix of embarrassment and arousal twisted in her chest. She lifted her fork and tried to take a bite, nodding her agreement that it was delicious, while her mind marveled at his laid-back demeanor and casual reference to their escapade at the restaurant.

He'd said they should talk after they ate. Somehow, she wasn't sure she could eat before they talked.

Phillip paused. "You don't like it?" He speared a zucchini off of her plate. "I know you don't like this."

"No, I do."

He swallowed the zucchini. "Then eat."

"I thought you mentioned that we were going to talk," she finally said with a forced, unemotional bravado.

"Right. We need to do that." He took another zucchini off of her plate.

She smacked his fork with hers. "Hey. Would you stop that and pay attention to what I said?"

"You said we need to talk. We're talking. But you're not going to eat this, right?" He held the vegetable up on the end of his fork then ate it without waiting a second.

Her need to talk about today stalled. "You remember I don't like zucchini?"

"The facts about Ashley Catherine Cartwright aren't hard to recall. Sweet, smart, great ass, and doesn't like zucchini."

It was such a small detail, but it clarified a harsh realization: losing Phillip was her biggest regret.

Her fork trembled, and she set it down. Nausea rolled through her, spreading her weakness from limb to limb.

"Hey." His gaze narrowed, and concern was inflected in his tone. "Are you okay?"

"I'm fine." She waved him back, nowhere near understanding what had happened today and how she felt. "Dehydrated, maybe."

Worry darkened his eyes, and he handed her the cool tumbler filled to the brim with water.

"Thanks." The water didn't help. She replayed every moment leading up to their encounter at the restaurant. Phillip had almost swung at Sean over the jab about his aunt and uncle. In the hallway, she had done what she'd needed to do to calm him down. But their tensions had already been so high, their anger toward one another maybe even higher, that when he'd kissed her, she couldn't hold back... and neither could he.

Her stomach dropped. They didn't have sex because they'd lost control and acted on impulse. Sex had been nothing more than a distraction. Phillip hadn't fought Sean nor fled the restaurant. He'd fucked her.

"I'm sorry, but I have to go." She stood unsteadily, not sure how to even get home. Her napkin tumbled down her legs, and she let it fall.

CHAPTER THIRTY-TWO

WHAT JUST HAPPENED? Phillip remained dumbstruck, staring at the hall that Ashley had disappeared into.

Then he started after her. Hell if he was going to let her leave like that. He found her by the front door, furiously texting. She didn't turn as he approached.

"Ashley."

Her brow tightened, but she didn't look up from the screen. "Mary Beth can pick me up."

"Ashley."

She stole a quick glance up, but Phillip couldn't decipher her distraught expression. *Lost? Angry? Filled with regret?* "I'll take you home."

Again, she studied her text messages as though they were vital to life and death. "Don't worry about it. It's okay."

He stepped closer. "Then tell her that you need a few minutes."

"I don't need a few minutes."

He closed the distance between them and covered her phone with his hand. "Ashley. You do."

Her chin jerked up, and her lips parted, but she didn't speak.

"*I* need a few minutes," he amended.

Slowly, she dropped her hands to her sides and put her phone into her purse. "She hadn't answered me."

"Come on." He lightly took her elbow and led her the opposite way from where they had come.

She fell into stride with him, easier than he had expected, but she asked, "Where are we going?"

"Somewhere that we can have privacy."

Without the barrage of expected questions, Ashley remained by his side as they went upstairs and entered his bedroom suite.

"I shouldn't be in here," she said.

He led her to the sitting area across from the bed and backed away. She needed space.

She eased into a matching chair an arm's length from him.

"You were right," he said. "We need to talk."

Earlier, he had planned to talk about work, specifically the things they hadn't gotten to the day before when they'd fought about Sean Paget.

Ashley shook her head. "No. I mean, yes, but downstairs... I'm fine."

His face skewed. "I can tell." Then Phillip sighed and ran his hand into his hair, slouching back. "About earlier—"

"Please don't," she whispered.

He had so much to say, so much he wanted to do. One taste of her hadn't been enough. He didn't know if time had healed his wounds, but he knew it hadn't dampened his feelings. Every interaction with Ashley pulled another layer away, bringing him closer to the way that he had cared for her long ago.

That was something he'd forgotten. He'd blocked out the loss of his lover and best friend, only hanging on to the lust and hurt pride. He'd known that he loved her, and now he continued to remember what they had actually been, what they could be—in love.

"We could talk about the car show," she suggested. "The Ferrari, maybe?"

The Ferrari hit him in the chest, though she had no idea. He ignored the memories of the best connection he had to his father. "There's nothing left to do for it. Our family accountants and lawyers already had me sign the needed paperwork."

"Oh, okay." The brief work conversation seemed to have given her strength. Then she ticked off her to-do list from memory.

As he listened, he realized that he was wrong. Work hadn't brought her back to life—it had just given her a safe topic to discuss. She did so in a mechanical fashion.

Phillip interrupted only to add what he'd already done and mentally took notes for her requests and ideas.

The back-and-forth slowed, and the work conversation wrapped until silence hung between them like a stormy cloud that had rolled back in.

Ashley stood. "So, we've talked."

He shook his head. "Not even close."

"Can we agree that earlier was a mistake?" Her quick words fell as her cheeks reddened.

"I don't think it was a mistake." He leaned back in the chair.

She cringed. "Come on, Phillip. We had a quickie—"

"We weren't anywhere near quick, beautiful."

"Phillip!"

His eyebrow arched. "Are you going to tell me that you disagree?"

She wouldn't meet his eye.

The stubborn frustration only egged him on. "Because I enjoyed myself and could've sworn you did too."

"Oh for God's sake."

He grinned, pleased her gaze met his, even if it was a glare. "I'll take that as a yes."

"You used me," she snapped.

His eyebrow cocked. That was an unexpected turn of the conversation. "Not any more than you used me."

"Not even close," she spat.

Phillip repositioned to sit next to her.

Ashley inched away. "You were pissed at me, at Sean." She folded her arms protectively around her purse. "You were ready to throw a punch when he brought up Graham and Claire."

He smirked. "I was there, thanks."

"You used sex to forget about everything!" She squeezed her bag and pivoted away.

Of all the accusations that Ashley could've lobbed at him... Phillip let that one roll through his thoughts. Uncomfortable situation and crazy behavior... The woman knew him too well, but she didn't have all of the facts.

"Normally..." He inhaled and held the breath while searching for the right words. They didn't come, and Phillip rubbed the back of his neck. "Yeah, normally, I'd say you're right."

Ashley twisted her head toward him. Weariness cloaked her face.

"I'd totally fuck to forget." He shrugged. "Seems like it's a win-win solution after lunch with that asshole."

She remained quiet, waiting, and turned another degree closer.

He shook his head. "But that wasn't what happened today."

"Of course it was," she whispered.

Phillip almost grinned. "How about a distant runner-up of a reason?" He pulled her close, though tension made her rigid under his touch. "Ashley, look at me."

Her chin lifted, and she stared at him, unblinking.

Phillip removed her purse from her clutches and set it on the ground. "Since we ran into each other, the need to be with you again has been all-consuming."

"All-consuming is a bit much."

"And today?" he continued. "You're right—I needed you. Wanted you. I used you, if that's what you want to call it. You make me feel like I can't fucking breathe until I'm inside of you."

She swallowed hard.

He didn't wait for her rebuttal. "Call that whatever you want. I needed you then like that. You demanding. Me happily, *savagely* delivering."

Her breath shook. "What do you need now?"

Phillip smiled. "I'm no less savage but maybe more controlled."

Arousal flared in her eyes as she bit her bottom lip.

"I can want you," Phillip said. "Need you." *Love you.* He faltered then shook away his shock. "In a hundred different ways. So long as I have you."

"I'm not sure what you want from me, and I really need to know."

He brushed her hair off her cheek. "Spend the night with me, and I'll show you."

CHAPTER THIRTY-THREE

"Y OU CAME HOME late last night." Mary Beth raised her eyebrows.

"Was it late?" Ashley tightened her robe over the oversized T-shirt she wore as pajamas and crossed the breakfast nook.

"You're glowing." Mary Beth sipped her tea then clucked. "And I haven't seen you in a few days."

Ashley couldn't hide her smile as she turned to her best friend. "I've had a few interesting days."

"I'd say so by that dopey grin and the small-but-noticeable-only-to-a-best-friend hickey on your neck."

Ashley slapped her hand over the spot on her neck that Phillip had spent an inordinate amount of time focused on.

Mary Beth leaned back in her chair, laughing. "And you even knew the spot where it might be. How very interesting."

Phillip's footsteps preceded him by a few seconds. Mary Beth cocked her head, not doing a thing to hide her surprise, or maybe it was glee. "And I can guess who the culprit might be?" She put her tea down and jumped up with her hand out before Ashley could make introductions. "You are the perfectly marvelous ex-boyfriend that I've heard so much about."

Phillip chuckled as Ashley groaned, watching her ex-boyfriend and best friend shake hands.

"I never called you perfectly marvelous." Ashley gave Mary Beth a snake eye then headed to make her morning tea.

"Oh," Mary Beth said with a mischievous laugh. "The

names she called you aren't fit to share."

Phillip snickered. "I can only imagine."

"I am ignoring the both of you," Ashley added.

"That's good because"—Mary Beth focused on Phillip— "I want to know if you're still considered an ex."

"Mary Beth!"

Mary Beth turned, arms out. "What? I'm talking to the man while wearing my emoji pajamas. I can ask him whatever I want to."

"Sounds fair to me," he said.

"Sounds like an abuse of the best friend handbook," Ashley disagreed. "Go find the rules. Thou shall not question—"

"Nope." Mary Beth grinned and shook her head. "I'm allowed to. The rule book says so right after the section about consequences for failure to notify a roommate about a slumber party." She tilted her head, adding dramatically, "But I guess I should cut her some slack. This is her first time engaging with an overnight guest."

Ashley was going to die of mortification.

"Is that so?" Phillip's crooked grin hung haphazardly on his amused face.

"All right, you two. I'm going to go and hide now. Good work, the both of you." But despite the hot blush running from her cheeks to her toes and the dangerous lack of caffeine, Ashley floated down the hall. There was something awesome about her best friend and her—whatever he was—getting along.

★　★　★

WITH TWO MUGS of green tea in hand, Phillip nudged the cracked bedroom door open with his foot. He held up the steaming mugs as a peace offering, chuckling when Ashley threw herself over the bed. "Don't mind me. I've suffered death by embarrassment."

He chuckled. "Nah." He set the mugs on the nightstand by her bed and sat on the edge. "That could have been a lot worse."

"Not your call to make. And why is she up?" Ashley threw her arms in the air then flopped back onto the bed. "She's never up this early."

"Well, I think it could have gone a lot worse. She could have thrown her bagel or coffee at me. I can only imagine the things that you've said."

She propped herself up against the headboard. Phillip passed her a mug then settled next to her. "I'm like the prodigal son—but the ex-boyfriend—returning again."

Ashley groaned and rolled her eyes. "I'd elbow you, but I don't want to spill my tea." She lifted a foot and hooked it over his legs, which were sprawled in front of him. The oversized T-shirt she wore slid up her thigh, and he laughed. "At least I was dressed."

He had put on his clothes from the day before. "Maybe you didn't realize I liked to walk around naked, letting it all hang out. That's a new fun fact about me."

Ashley snorted. "Mary Beth would have died."

Ashley grinned, then carefully sipped from her mug. He took it from her hands and sat it next to his untouched tea.

"Hey," she complained.

"Taking your morning caffeine is a dangerous move, but I'm going to risk it."

Her lips quirked. "Only if you know what you're doing."

Ha. Not really. He was flying by the seat of his pants, which was ironic since he had formed a plan to win her back. He hadn't come close to even nailing the first step. Instead, he'd jumped ahead and then fallen back to the start again. There had been no order, yet there they were.

"Mary Beth asked you a question," he pointed out. *Was the ex-boyfriend still the ex?*

Ashley's lips rounded. "Well, um…"

Her answer was his too. How much of their old relationship still needed to be addressed? Maybe none at all. Maybe he should admit how close he'd come to proposing. Hell, maybe not. "Yeah, those are exactly my thoughts too," he teased.

She laughed. "What's that mean?"

Draping his arm around her, Phillip pulled Ashley close and kissed the top of her head. "No more exes."

"Is it that simple?"

"Of course. You're mine, and that makes me yours."

CHAPTER THIRTY-FOUR

"Easy." Phillip signaled for the transport crew to back the donation car from Mr. Paget off the flatbed truck. The ground crew moved quickly to secure it to rollers then move the '55 Mercedes-Benz 300CL Gullwing onto the raised platform for the car show's center stage. Once the car was in place, Phillip gave a thumbs-up. "Perfect."

Footsteps echoed behind him, and Phillip turned.

"That's right. A million dollars of classic, lightweight German perfection." Robert Paget ambled toward them with a grand smile. Next to him was his son Sean.

Inwardly, Phillip groaned, but he kept his focus on the roadster as the ground crew positioned it and opened its iconic doors, hinged along the roof. When he was certain he had his cool, Phillip greeted the older Paget.

"She's a beauty, isn't she?" Robert clapped his hands together, appreciating the car. "I can't say it won't hurt to see this one go, but she was an investment." He stopped next to Phillip, and they shook hands before continuing. "And this one will pay off nicely, with the bonus of a fat tax relief. You can't beat that. Can you?"

"No, sir. You can't," Phillip agreed as he greeted Sean with the same nod that Sean had given him. They had avoided phone calls and meetings since the incident at the restaurant, and Phillip had never been so happy for the existence of text messages and emails.

Robert gestured between them. "I'm glad to see you two

work together so well. Charity was never something I spent enough time on, and it means a great deal to see my boy lifting that weight."

Sean remained close-lipped but offered an amicable nod of agreement. Phillip wasn't so sure that he was able to maintain that level of composure.

Robert turned back to his car. "Now that she's here, I'm ready to sign her off of my hands. Show me the forms, and then I have to run."

With little small talk, Phillip led them to the main building. He and Ashley had commandeered a meeting room and turned it into their nerve center for the final day before and after the auction. But she was nowhere to be seen. A Post-It note was stuck to his screen with Ashley's script. *Bitsy called. I'm headed to meet her and Mary Beth. Be back in an hour. Or maybe three. Who knows?* She signed off with a heart and the letter A.

Perhaps Bitsy had some kind of magic ability to show up and interrupt when needed. Either way, Ashley's disappearance worked well with Sean's unexpected arrival.

Phillip removed a folder and presented it to Robert with a pen. He pulled out the form inside the folder and read the acknowledgment of delivery, requiring that they both sign. He removed a Montblanc pen from his jacket pocket and signed with a quick scrawl. Phillip used his pen to countersign.

"Check that box. Everything on my end is done." Robert clapped a hand on Phillip's back. "Don't forget to ask me to participate again next year."

Wow, things had changed in the course of a few weeks, from Robert wanting nothing to do with him to volunteering for next year already. All Phillip could do was nod. "Yes, sir."

As the father gestured to his son, Sean said, "I need a few minutes with Phillip. You don't have to wait. I can find my own ride."

Tension ticked deep within Phillip. The unreadable man

seemed ready to make a move, and Phillip wanted to see what would come of it.

After a quick back-and-forth, Robert departed. The echo of his loafers drifted away before Sean and Phillip turned to face each other. The anticipation forced the hairs on the back of his neck to stand up.

He noticed how Sean's jaw ticked and how the corners of his mouth tightened.

The room crackled with competition and anger. Soon they would collide unless Phillip broke the tension. He refused to react to his adrenaline or to Sean. Not waiting for Sean to make a move, Phillip dove into the conversation. "About Montgomery's." He shifted, forcing himself to maintain complete control. "You picked up the tab."

Sean nodded. "I didn't need to stick around after Ashley left with you."

Phillip's molars ground as he recalled Sean's accusation about Graham and Claire that had set off the events. Right now, that was all Phillip could focus on, not giving a damn about how long they'd been gone or what Sean might assume.

"I was out of line," Sean admitted then cleared his throat. "I tend to view people as a mean to an end. Maybe you can relate. The family business is the only life I know."

"No, I cannot."

Sean pursed his lips. "Well, that makes two of you, because neither can Ashley."

Phillip didn't move, waiting for Sean to explain what he meant or get the hell out.

"But," Sean started, "Agatha Cartwright is another story."

Phillip's molars clamped tighter, and his pulse thumped in his temples. "Ashley and her mother are nothing alike, and that's a good thing in my book."

Sean lifted his shoulders. "In her own weird way, Agatha is doing what she thinks is best for Ashley." Sean tucked his hands into the pockets of his pressed khaki pants. "But I'm not what's best for Ashley."

"No shit."

Sean snorted. "I guess you can see that pretty clearly, but it took her looking at you when I was being a jackass to see there was something there." Again Sean cleared his throat, his discomfort becoming clearer with every word. "My point is this. I was out of line, doing Agatha's bidding, with the incentive of a connection with the Cartwrights."

"You don't need a merger of families to succeed," Phillip managed between sealed teeth.

Sean shook his head. "Spoken like a true billionaire who wants for nothing."

"You have no idea about me."

"I don't know how much of a difference a few hundred million versus a billion makes." Sean paced the length of the small makeshift office and stopped in front of a row of promotional gift bags. Fliers were stacked in each, and he pulled the heavy glossy paper out. It was an informational sheet on Phillip's nonprofit. The top of the promo featured a group of kids at his camp, huddled together for the camera. The text underneath explained how they'd all lost their families. Sean read the front, then flipped the paper and put it back into the bag. "Maybe you're right. Maybe I don't know you."

The door opened. Ashley and Mary Beth bounced in. Their energetic conversation choked silent.

"Ashley, I'm glad you're here," Sean said, walking from the gift bags.

Color drained from her face, and before Phillip could reassure her that all would be okay, Sean continued. "I owe you an apology."

Phillip stopped abruptly. Mary Beth's eyes rounded, but Ashley's shocked expression fell prey to her impeccable manners. Her color snapped back as she simultaneously accepted the apology and explained that it wasn't needed.

Mary Beth beckoned for Phillip as she backed toward the door. "I think that we need to check on the—"

Ashley caught Mary Beth by the arm, preventing her escape. Even if she had left, Phillip had no intention of going anywhere.

Sean took a step closer to Ashley. "I should have let you know that I planned to come to King Harbor to meet with your mother, but it didn't occur to me. I was in a business frame of mind."

"She called you?" Ashley asked him quietly.

He nodded. "She did."

Her fingers flexed into Mary Beth's arm, and Phillip contained a protective urge to end the conversation.

"What did she say?" she asked.

"Not much."

Apparently, that was the wrong thing to say. Ashley marched forward, morphing from uncertain to pissed. "Tell me what she said."

Phillip stepped between Ashley and Sean. "Easy. Take a breath."

"She deserves to know," Sean said.

Phillip was never sure about anything to do with her mother.

"He might be right, Phillip," Mary Beth said.

He hadn't put this to a vote, damn it. But he was outnumbered and wearily stepped an inch back, still hovering close in case Ashley forgot those manners her mother had drilled into her and decided to slug Sean. Someone had to be close enough to ice his girl's hand.

Sean offered a flat, thin-lipped expression. "I wasn't looking for romance when we met. I was in business mode, and I wanted a wife."

Ashley's lips parted as she sucked in a small gasp.

"And I knew that you didn't want that role before you ended things. But I'm a man, and you're gorgeous—"

"Watch yourself," Phillip interrupted.

Sean seemed to grasp where the line of appropriateness was drawn. He continued. "But it needs to be said. I was either interested in gratification, or…"

"A business merger," Ashley supplied without parting her teeth.

Sean nodded. "To be perfectly up-front, yes." Then he turned his focus to Phillip, adding, "Of which, you gave me neither."

"Good thing," Mary Beth mumbled.

Sean turned from Phillip to Ashley. "I'm not doing a good job of explaining myself. But you have to understand that I didn't come to Ashley with false intentions. I was operating with bad information."

"From my mother?" Ashley asked.

"Yes. But truthfully, I don't think she understands you," Sean gently offered.

"That would be an understatement," Phillip muttered.

Ashley jerked away.

"Ashley, look. I speak her language," Sean said. "In her own way, your mother is trying." He pulled an easier breath as though this was something he understood. "Not all people see relationships the same way. My point in this whole explanation is that I'm sorry for stepping into this situation when I had no business being here." He turned back to Phillip. "Even now, I think that you're one hell of a lucky man." Sean extended his hand, waiting for Phillip's move.

In that moment, Phillip saw how different things could have gone. He could have punched Sean at Montgomery's, proving to Ashley that emotions dictated his behavior. Besides embarrassing the Blackthorne name again, he would've missed out on a scorching-hot makeup session.

And Phillip remained in control with Sean, without her to run interference. Understanding and apologies had come about. He shook Sean's hand, then they said their goodbyes.

As the other man walked out, Phillip pulled Ashley under his arm and into his chest.

"I have someplace else to be." Mary Beth followed Sean out.

Phillip breathed Ashley in. If he could make it through the car show, while winning his woman and watching the auction of his beloved car without losing his mind, Phillip was certain that nothing would ruin their love. Except...

His stomach sank. Ashley hadn't been privy to the discussion *he'd* had with her mother. Given what they'd learned today, he wasn't sure if she should ever know.

CHAPTER THIRTY-FIVE

DESPITE THE UNEXPECTED personal drama, Ashley breezed through the last-minute items on her to-do list. Gift bags had been stuffed. Tables were ready for vendors to arrive at dawn. She'd checked and rechecked her list. "I'm so excited for tomorrow."

"Yup." Phillip tapped a pen on the desk as he stared at what looked like the same pile of papers that held his attention for the last twenty minutes.

"That sounded convincing."

His shoulders bunched. "I am."

If she didn't know that even the smallest details for their event were handled, she would've guessed a problem loomed. "Is everything okay?"

His pen tapped faster. "Uh-huh."

She moved and peeked over his shoulder and read the description given to the auctioneer for the Ferrari 330 GT. "Is that on your mind?"

Phillip took a look as though he hadn't realized what was in front of him. "No." He sighed and pinched the bridge of his nose. "But I'll admit, the closer tomorrow comes, the heavier this loss feels."

Her forehead bunched. "I thought you didn't like that car."

He pursed his lips. "Not exactly."

She sat on the edge of the desk. "Then what?"

His stormy expression furrowed. "It was the last gift my

dad gave me."

"Oh…"

"He enjoyed working on his favorite cars, and I think it was supposed to be a shared hobby. Something to keep me out of trouble, I guess." His lips thinned. "It didn't work."

"What do you mean?"

Phillip shrugged. "I still caused enough trouble for them to send me to wilderness camp."

She knew the story from there. He hadn't shared much about losing his parents, but Ashley had known about the crash on the way to pick him up. "You don't have to auction it off."

He brushed her off. "I do."

"*No*, you don't. You don't have to do anything—"

"I appreciate that, but it's listed in the program—"

"So what!" She stood. "Donations change all the time."

He grinned softly. "I appreciate that, and as many memories as the Ferrari holds, I'd like to see it raise money for the camp."

"Phillip…" She could raise money for the camp in another way. He could even buy it at his own auction! That was the bonus of being a billionaire.

He took her hand. "That wasn't what was on my mind, but I'm glad I told you." With a quick squeeze, he turned for the desk, flipping to another page of notes for the auctioneer.

Ashley stood behind him and rested her hands on his shoulders. He was a ball of stress, and sharing about his car hadn't helped. She kneaded his tight muscles. "Do you want to tell me what else is wrong?"

"I think that's all the hard-hitting confessions I can handle tonight."

Her curiosity piqued at the prospect of something that emotionally charged. She wanted to press but held back. He asked for room, and she would give it. Ashley leaned down and rested her chin at the crook of his neck. "There's nothing left to do. Let's go home. We'll meet again bright and early."

"I wish you'd come home with me tonight." His voice rumbled as though he needed more than her naked in his bed.

She wanted to whisper that everything would be fine and hold him until he knew that to be true. "I need to get ready at home."

"I have a shower," he offered.

"It's late, and I haven't picked out what I'm going to wear, much less which accessories."

"You got me on accessories." Phillip stretched back in the office chair. His tired eyes and drained expression had her curling into his lap.

She nuzzled against his chest. "We can cuddle here for a few minutes. Maybe you'll feel better."

He stroked the back of her hair then sighed. "Probably not until I get something off my chest."

She glanced up, wondering what his hard-hitting revelation would be.

"It doesn't do either of us any good, but I think you should know."

She laid her cheek down again and let the steady rhythm of his heartbeat quiet her growing alarm. "If you want to share…"

"I had a conversation with your mother also," he admitted quietly.

She tensed. "A conversation like Mother had with Sean?"

His hair-stroking stopped, and Phillip cupped the back of her neck as if she might pull away. "Do you remember the weekend your parents came to Cambridge, before your mother was the dean's special guest?"

The weekend before she broke up with him. Her stomach lurched, and Ashley lifted her chin.

He pressed his forehead to hers. "I met your parents for breakfast."

"No, we didn't."

"*I* met your parents for breakfast."

Uncertainty blossomed. "I don't understand."

He inched back, and his gaze darkened. "I told them that I loved you."

She choked. "What?"

He swallowed hard. "And that it was my intention to marry you one day."

Memories of her parents' visit to Harvard clouded her mind. Mother had spoken of Ashley's future in her company and the sky-high expectations for her class presentation. She vividly recalled Mother's offhand remarks about Phillip's reputation for irresponsibility and recklessness, as well as her unsought advice for Ashley to break up with him. Ashley also clearly remembered painfully seeking her mother's approval. "What—" Her voice cracked, and she cleared her throat. "What did they say?"

His sad, helpless grin broke her heart. "They gave me their blessing."

CHAPTER THIRTY-SIX

ASHLEY BLARED THE car radio on her drive home. The noise hadn't helped drown her anger. By the time she'd pulled onto her street, she'd reached dangerous levels of self-loathing and fury. If she'd been a stronger person. If her mother actually cared for her. If, if, if—she wanted to scream!

For the first time, she was glad that her mother was staying in the guest bedroom. There were a few things they needed to discuss. Ashley sped into the driveway and slammed the brakes hard enough for her seat belt to jerk.

She stormed toward the confrontation that had been years in the making. Her hands trembled as she fumbled for her keys before giving up and smacking the front door. It was less of a knock, and more a feeble attempt to knock it down.

The door swung open, and Mary Beth gaped from the other side. "Are you okay?"

"Where is she?" Ashley blew by. "Where is my mother?"

"She's gone." Mary Beth shut the door.

Ashley spun. "She left?"

Mary Beth nodded. "What's wrong?"

"I'm going to kill her."

"What happened?"

"I don't know where to begin." Ashley whirled toward the dining room and threw her purse and keys onto the table. "I've always known she pulled the strings in my life. There was a time that I let her."

"But not anymore," Mary Beth assured.

"It doesn't matter. There are always consequences." A flood of tears brimmed in her eyes.

"What happened this time?"

It was more than Ashley could fathom explaining. "Phillip."

A quizzical look crossed Mary Beth's face. "Something happened after I left?"

"No. A long time ago." Ashley closed her eyes as devastation rolled over her, momentarily covering her rage. She thought about all that they had missed. "I'm going to be sick."

Mary Beth followed Ashley to the bathroom. Ashley collapsed onto the floor, half certain that she would vomit, half ready to sob. "I broke up with him for the pettiest reasons."

Mary Beth scrunched her lips. "I don't know. A goat? You wanted someone stable and responsible."

"I wanted love!" Ashley dropped her head into her hands. "Phillip met with my parents and told them that he planned to marry me."

Ashley hazarded a look up when Mary Beth didn't respond. Her jaw simply hung.

"I messed up."

Mary Beth wrapped Ashley in her arms and hugged tightly.

She sobbed, furious and never feeling more like a fool. "I'm so stupid."

"Not stupid," Mary Beth whispered. "Just full of regret."

Ashley leaned back. "I don't know how he can even look at me. And it gets worse."

"What else did she do?" Mary Beth asked, her tone as cold as ice.

"Ha. Not her. It was me." Ashley blew her nose into a tissue and threw it into the trash can. "I asked him to donate a car—it was the most expensive one I knew he had. I thought he hated it, that it would bring a lot of money in for the charities."

"So?"

"That car was a gift from his father for them to bond over, but they never finished it before his parents died."

Tears brimmed in Mary Beth's eyes. "Oh God."

"I know." Another round of hot tears stung Ashley's cheeks. "He signed the contract to give it away, and it's one of the main... It's *the* main draw for tomorrow. Bidders have come in from out of state."

"So what? He can take it back."

Ashley slowly shook her head. "He has convinced himself that it would be a nice full-circle gesture for the funds to go to his camp."

"It's hard to argue with reasons like that." Mary Beth chewed her cheeks. "Set the donation part aside. Does he want to keep the car?"

"He didn't say as much, but I think so."

She hummed. "What are you going to do?"

"I have no idea." Ashley wiped her face off then sat on the edge of the tub. "I could always try to buy it during the auction."

"And I can start a whisper campaign amongst the bidders," Mary Beth offered hopefully. "If anyone tries for it, we'll just sic Bitsy on them."

Ashley laughed even as she shook her head. "I don't want to ruin the event. His charity gets a lot of money from this, and I would never be able to compete with other bidders. Plus, he'd stop me."

Mary Beth brightened. "Wait. There are anonymous bidders. You could be one of those."

Ashley paused and let her wheels turn. "That's true." But her hope dimmed. "I don't have enough cash in bank."

"If you're serious, maybe there's something you could sell? List as collateral?"

"Hmm." Ashley had her house. Big-dollar bidding wasn't

her cup of tea, and she had no idea how to facilitate such a deal. "If I could figure out how, I would sell this place tonight."

"Well…" Mary Beth tapped her teeth and thought. "It's worth reminding you, we do live here."

"We can move someplace that Mother can't just show up at."

Mary Beth remained unconvinced. "Forget that we live here. This house holds significance to you. It's not like you have a lot of cherished family mementos."

That was true. But nothing compared to what that car meant to Phillip. Ashley could hold on to her grandmother's memory in a different way.

Mary Beth kneeled so that they were eye-to-eye. "Maybe you should slow down and think about what you're suggesting. You two just became a thing again."

"It doesn't matter. I love him."

CHAPTER THIRTY-SEVEN

AFTER A CUP of decaf tea with Mary Beth, a plan to sell the house overnight hadn't materialized. But Ashley had tempered the frenzied need to save Phillip's car and instead picked out her clothing and accessories for tomorrow.

Sleep called, but she couldn't lie down in bed. Her thoughts spiraled over Mother orchestrating the conversation with Sean but then leaving King Harbor before Ashley could confront her.

"Always calling the shots," Ashley muttered, wondering if she should call Mother and yell. Though it wouldn't change anything. Ashley wondered what her father might do if she asked him to pick a side and defend her. Did he know that Mother didn't want Phillip in Ashley's life? He had to care. He'd been the more nurturing parent—at least, when he was home.

Suddenly, she needed to hear from her dad and grabbed the phone. Without giving herself a moment to chicken out, Ashley scrolled to her parents' names and hit send.

Dad didn't answer. Disappointed, but not deterred from the confrontation, she decided on a video chat with her mother.

She hit the icon to connect, and as it started to ring, she realized she didn't know what to say. Nothing beyond irate accusations formed coherently as the call connected.

Her mother appeared on the screen, and from the background, Ashley could tell that the call had been accepted from her iPad in the living room. "It's late," her mother said as greeting, then inched closer to the screen and took a long look. "Is something wrong?"

"Yes." Ashley inhaled slowly, struggling to maintain an even tone. "Is Dad there?"

"Are you sick?"

"Ask Dad to join you, please," she said, then hated how she'd tacked on *please*. "It's important."

Her mother frowned then rose from the chair. Her silk robe and matching nightgown flowed as she left the living room.

Mother finally returned with Ashley's pajama-clad father. They sat in front of the screen, and with a hint of concern, her father asked, "Is everything okay?"

She realized that she hadn't heard any concern from her mother. Then she realized that she wasn't surprised. Ashley swallowed hard. "Phillip asked you if he could marry me." She had meant it to come out as a question, but she knew it to be fact.

Her mother braced a hand to her chest.

"Phillip Blackthorne? From Harvard?" her dad asked, confused.

"Did I date any other Phillips?"

Her father crooked his head, seeming to acknowledge her emotional tone. "Yes. Phillip spoke with us. But that was…" He faltered. "Years ago."

Tears stung the back of her throat. "Why didn't you say anything?"

Dad shifted uncomfortably. They weren't a talk-about-feelings family.

"Well, honey…" Dad glanced at her mother, frozen and growing pale. His gaze narrowed quizzically, but he continued. "You broke up with him and seemed so distraught."

Perplexed concern marred his face. Ashley compared it to her mother, who remained unmoved. "You didn't know, did you, Dad?"

"Know what?"

She could barely look at her mother. "It was 100 percent your doing." Deep down, had she hoped to discover a misunderstanding?

Dad's brows furrowed and glanced again at her mother. "What is going on?"

"I think we've had enough excitement for one night." Her mother stood. "Have a good event tomorrow—"

Ashley slapped her palm against the table. "Sit down."

"Watch your tone, young lady," her mother warned.

"Aggi, what the hell is going on?"

No one gave him an answer.

"Sit down, and we'll figure this out," he commanded. "Agatha."

Robotically, her mother returned to the couch next to her dad.

"Thank you," Dad said. "Will someone tell me what the hell is going on?"

"I can," Ashley said. "I was weak and a fool, and at the time, there was no one in the world whose approval I needed more than my mother."

Dad stared at her hard and then turned to her mother. "What does that mean?"

After a silent standoff between her parents, her mother stiffly rejoined them. "I did it for your own good."

Dad's brows furrowed. "Hell, Aggi, what did you do?"

"I explained that she had found the wrong Blackthorne." Her lips trembled though she lifted her chin. "That she had the right type of family that would be a good match, but that Phillip was irresponsible, embarrassing, and would ruin her future—all of which was true."

Dad's head dropped. He rubbed the bridge of his nose. "Damn it. We decided to let her make her own decisions." He glanced up. "This is why you didn't take the job?"

"With Mother?" Ashley nodded. "I didn't know how much manipulation there had been, but I knew that I didn't trust myself around her."

"I had your best interest at heart," Mother added quietly with an unexpected hint of emotion.

Ashley shook her head. "You say that like you haven't been interfering now with Sean Paget."

"Well…" Mother's shoulders slumped.

Dad turned, disappointed. "Really?" A long, unsaid conversation transpired between her parents, leaving Ashley to wonder how much Mother's actions had been a problem between them. Finally, Dad faced the screen again. "Honey, you need to know that we both love you."

"Love or not, meaning well or not, actions have consequences. I lost Phillip—I convinced him to donate a car from his father." She choked up. "Never mind, I have to go."

"Wait," Dad said.

"Ashley, I am…" Her mother cleared her throat. "I'm—I shouldn't have interfered."

"It's late." Her dad rubbed the back of his neck. "You have a big day tomorrow, but we will continue this conversation." He cleared his throat. "It's time we do that more often, and we will. But for now, honey, get some sleep."

CHAPTER THIRTY-EIGHT

PHILLIP AMBLED THROUGH the parking lot lined with classic cars, hot rods, and antiques. He took a long look at a 1965 Shelby Cobra. Its white paint and cherry-red leather seats were enticing, and he took the owner's business card.

He caught Ashley's eye as she stood, unable to get away from a '69 Chevelle. Phillip laughed, having already been caught by the owner who wouldn't let anyone pass without hearing his nightmare of an internet purchase. Sight unseen, the Chevelle rolled off a flatbed in his driveway with a box of unrelated parts where a 454 Chevy engine should've been.

"Excuse me," Phillip interrupted. "A small emergency has popped up."

After a quick round of small talk, they made their escape.

"You owe me." He tucked her under his arm.

"I'll buy you a snow cone," she offered as they passed a little girl with a blue face, holding a half-eaten cone.

"Sounds fair." They worked their way through the maze of restored cars, and Phillip greeted familiar faces that supported his nonprofit year after year.

They reached the snow cone table, appreciated the quick line, and turned toward a stage where the band played for the afternoon sock hop. "The Laumet ladies are in the zone."

"All's well that ends well," she said.

But Phillip couldn't quite catch her tone. Her smile was firmly in place, though something seemed wrong. "Are you having fun?"

She nodded, crunching into the snow cone. "Though I wouldn't mind if it were just a few degrees cooler."

The asphalt didn't help the heat. "Why don't you go inside and cool down?" She could take a minute off her feet in their office. "Or do another check of everything for tonight."

Her grin tightened. "That's a good idea. I'll do that."

She popped onto her toes and kissed his cheek goodbye. Smiles and smooches aside, he still wondered if something was wrong.

"Everything looks great."

Phillip turned, not expecting to see Hannah, Devlin, and Brock. "What are you doing here?"

Hannah tilted her head as though his question were Greek. "We're enjoying everything King Harbor has to offer."

"It's about time I showed up at this thing," Brock added.

"Oh, I think I see someone I know." Hannah pointed toward a gaggle eating kettle corn and left without saying goodbye.

"Must've been an important person," Brock muttered.

Devlin shook his head. "We could've planned that a little better."

Phillip looked between his brother and cousin, wondering what was going on. "Plan what?"

Devlin and Brock exchanged glances. "We talked."

"This doesn't sound good." Phillip backed up to a trash can and ditched his untouched snow cone. Returning, he crossed his arms. "I'm ready. Whatever it is."

They laughed.

"We're going to buy the Ferrari," Devlin said. "Everyone will kick in some cash, and it'll be like a gift and a donation."

"That was my idea." Brock grinned before Phillip could register what they'd said. "I know there are a couple things that you never got to with Dad."

A wave of emotion hit him, and Phillip's throat tied into a knot.

"I was too young to pick up anything from Dad," Brock added. "And you need to know I don't blame you for that."

Phillip swallowed hard. He'd lived a lifetime certain that Brock blamed him for their deaths. The weight of the conversation nearly made him cry, but he managed to crack, "Since when do you fix up cars?"

Brock chuckled. "I thought maybe you could show me a thing or two, big brother, or even better, we just look at it and sip whisky."

Big brother hit Philip in the gut. One double whammy after another. He was certain Brock didn't see him in the role of an oldest brother.

Phillip rubbed a hand over his face. "I appreciate the gesture, guys, but really, don't."

"Come on." Devlin tilted his head. "The family's on board."

"We want you to keep the car." Brock stepped back, and Uncle Graham joined the conversation, greeting Phillip with a nod.

This was like an intervention.

"We do." Uncle Graham drew their attention. "And I need to make a correction to what I said before. You are every bit the Blackthorne you should be. I'm sorry if I said anything to the contrary."

He didn't know what to say.

"Don't give up the car if it's only to bring the Blackthorne name good press," his uncle added.

God, he loved his family, the whole stubborn lot of them. They were all the same, in their own way. Blackthorne through and through. "I appreciate that—"

"But?" Brock crossed his arms.

Phillip chewed the inside of his cheek. "Following through is the right thing to do. Dad wanted me to grow up, to stand by my word, and that's what I've done."

CHAPTER THIRTY-NINE

T HE FERRARI 330 GT wouldn't be the most expensive car to go on the auction block that night. But it was the only one that paralyzed Ashley. Her banker approved a middle-of-the-night request for a line of credit, so long as she used her home as collateral.

The bank wire came through an hour before the auctioneer announced Phillip's Ferrari, and she couldn't breathe.

Ashley had empowered Mary Beth to sign her up as an anonymous bidder. She'd told her best friend how much she could spend and hid from Phillip. If he knew, he would make her stop. But if he got the car back, maybe she could make up for the hurt she'd caused in the past.

The auctioneer finished reading the description of the Ferrari 330 GT, and with great fanfare, he started the bidding with fast-flying words. "The auction's on. What are you going to give for it? Would you give one hundred thousand?"

Bidding paddles flew up.

"I've got a hundred." The auctioneer pointed toward the far corner. "Now a hundred and a quarter." He recognized another bidder.

A man in the front row raised his paddle. "Two fifty."

"Now," the auctioneer chanted, "Two seventy-five." He acknowledged another bidder. "Three and a quarter?"

The auctioneer's words flew. The bids rose higher and higher. After four hundred thousand dollars, bidders bowed out, and Ashley was near done.

"Anyone else? Four fifty?"

"Four fifty," the front row bidder called.

"Four seventy-five." The auctioneer gestured to the few remaining bidders. "Four seventy-five?"

Tears flooded her eyes. When her cell phone rang, she knew it would be Mary Beth.

Ashley answered, heartbroken. "I'm done."

"I understand," Mary Beth said, then hung up.

A second later, the woman who must've been her anonymous bidder said, "No, Colonel."

"Five hundred," another bidder called.

"Five twenty-five," the auctioneer chanted. "Will you give me five fifteen? Five fifteen? And... *sold* for five hundred thousand dollars."

Tears fell as an arm wrapped around Ashley's shoulder. "Phillip!" She clung to him as he dropped a kiss on the top of her head.

"It's okay," he promised, defeated. "Let's wrap up and go home."

★   ★   ★

THE DRIVE TO the Blackthorne estate was quiet, and Ashley wished a magic cure of explanation, apologies, and hope for the future would come together. But she didn't know what to say.

They arrived home, and Phillip slumped in the driver's seat. Asking what was wrong felt trivial. She couldn't imagine his loss and disappointment. Those years he'd told her that he hated the Ferrari... He'd hated losing his parents.

Ashley struggled to understand how she would feel. Her parents were so different, but if they were gone tomorrow, she would grieve. Even for her mother.

Phillip laced his fingers with hers. "Ready to go in?"

"Yes. But I want to say something first."

He squeezed her hand.

"I didn't take the position in my mother's company because... I didn't trust myself."

He shifted in the leather seat.

"There are things that I should have done differently, things that I should never have said. I never hated you, Phillip. It was a poor excuse that I held onto in my head." She sighed. "You told me about the conversation with my parents, and well, I didn't know I had the other side of the story. Either way, I don't want to keep anything from you."

"Secrets doom relationships," he said. "We don't want to end up like Uncle Graham and Aunt Claire."

Her heart soared that he could picture them together that far in the future. "We don't."

He took her hand.

"At Harvard, I let Mother get into my head, and at the time, I couldn't see any other way. All I wanted was her approval, and I turned away from you when you were exactly what I needed most."

He squeezed her hand. The interior lights had long since dimmed, and the moonlight provided a pale, shimmering glow. "I love you, Ashley. I loved you then. I love you now. Time and space haven't changed that I want to spend the rest of my life with you." He brought her knuckles to his lips and pressed a long kiss against them.

Tears, the first happy ones in ages, slid down her cheeks. "I never stopped loving you either."

CHAPTER FORTY

PHILLIP RAN HIS thumb over Ashley's knuckles as they walked into the front entryway of the estate. Lights and conversation radiated from the living room.

"I guess we'll say hello before bed," he said.

Uncle Graham and Nana relaxed on the couch with a bottle of Blackthorne Gold perched on the coffee table. They each held two fingers worth of whisky in crystal glasses. A third, empty glass waited next to a whisky bottle. "We should've known to expect you two." Uncle Graham stood, introducing himself to Ashley.

Phillip kissed Nana on the cheek. "There's someone I'd like to introduce you to." He put his hand on Ashley's back. "Mrs. Fiona Blackthorne, my girlfriend, Ashley Cartwright." He noticed his uncle's nod of clarification of what Ashley meant to Phillip. "Ashley, this is my lovely grandmother."

Nana stood and took Ashley by the shoulders. "Call me Fiona. These boys like to make me sound like an old bitty. It's 'cause I can drink them under the table."

They laughed, and Uncle Graham stepped to the side. "I'll get another glass."

"Thanks, Uncle Graham. But I think we're going to turn in."

"Take a minute and have a drink." Nana shooed her son to get Ashley's glass.

Once Phillip and Ashley were given their glasses, and all were seated around the coffee table, Nana offered, "*Slàinte mhath.*"

"*Slàinte mhath,*" Phillip cheered, adding for Ashley, "Good health and a happy life."

She grinned. "*Slann-Gaur-Vaer.*"

"Close enough," Nana decreed.

Laughing, he took a long, slow swig and let the smooth whisky slide down. Then he stood, ready to say good night.

Uncle Graham raised his hand. "One more thing."

He couldn't handle many more "one more things" this evening. But Phillip respectfully, if not exhaustedly, dropped back into his seat.

"I had a short phone call with Agatha Cartwright today," Uncle Graham said.

"My mother?" Ashley gasped. "Is everything okay?"

Of course it wasn't. Phillip knew better. Anytime Agatha Cartwright was involved, problems would arise.

"No, actually." Uncle Graham's eyes clouded, and his jaw went taut. "She explained that she'd misstepped in a conversation with Sean Paget."

Phillip's jaw tightened.

"It seems she had an opinion of a private matter between Claire and I." Uncle Graham's lips thinned, and Phillip cursed his uncle's stubborn streak that kept him from chasing down the woman he loved. "Don't worry about it, Uncle Graham. We didn't give it any thought."

"None," Ashley confirmed.

"Either way, you should know it's untrue," Uncle Graham said. "And that's all I'm going to say about that."

Nana snorted. "You forgave Agatha Cartwright so easily."

"Mother," Uncle Graham warned.

She ignored him, flipping her hand. "But go ahead and take all the time you need to clean up your own house. Such a *crabbit* of a man."

Uncle Graham finished the last of his drink. "Good night, Mother."

Phillip watched as his uncle walked away, noticing for the hundredth time that his step had slowed since Aunt Claire had had enough and left them all.

"Graham and Claire will be okay," Nana said. Then she muttered into her whisky, "As soon as they pull themselves together."

Phillip hoped so but was too tired to worry about them tonight. He gave Nana a kiss good night. "Don't stay up too late."

"Good night, dear." Nana shook her hand at Phillip. "All of them jealous that they can't keep up with their little old nana."

"That's the absolute truth." Phillip took Ashley's hand and led her through the quiet house to his bedroom.

Once inside, Ashley turned and waited for him to finish closing the door. "Does anyone really know what happened?"

That was a question Phillip had asked himself many times. "Between Uncle Graham and Aunt Claire? The secret?" He put his hands on her hips, inching them close together. "Nana knows everything about everything."

"Do you believe what she said?" Ashley snaked her hands around his neck and leaned against his chest.

They swayed as if slow dancing, and Phillip sighed. "I don't know if it matters. And Claire needed something that she couldn't find here." Admitting that hurt. It wasn't just between her and Uncle Graham. How hadn't he noticed that she'd felt ignored? He shrugged. "I hope she finds what she needs."

"I love you," Ashley whispered then brushed her lips across his. "Let's not be like that."

He grinned into her kiss. "Not even when we're old and gray."

CHAPTER FORTY-ONE

Ashley woke with a slumberous grin. A new day was upon them. A new chapter together, ready to unfold. She didn't know what exact steps would come next, but she knew to trust in them.

The weight of Phillip's muscular arm tightened around her waist. "Good morning, beautiful."

"This might be my favorite good morning ever," she admitted.

He rolled over on top of her. "I wonder how high I can move that bar."

Before she had a chance to respond, her cell phone rang across the room. After it stopped, it began ringing again, and her eyebrows rose.

"It's Bitsy," Phillip teased. "She wants to hang out and gossip."

The text message notification buzzed, and Ashley's happy morning turned in her stomach. "Maybe something's wrong." She scrambled from bed, wearing Phillip's T-shirt, which draped to her thighs as she raced to her phone. It only took a few seconds for her to come up with a list of possible disasters. Who would call and text if there wasn't a problem? Finally, she found her phone at the bottom of her purse. "It's Mary Beth!"

The text message notification preview popped up.

SOS. Answer your phone!

"Oh God, something is wrong." Ashley dialed her best friend back.

Mary Beth answered immediately. "You need to come home. Now."

"What? Why?"

"Your mother is here—without her people—but she brought your father in tow."

KEEPING THE PORSCHE under the speed limit had never been a problem for Phillip. If he wanted speed, he would do it with intention.

But he was feeling was a different kind of energy that tempted him to lean into the gas pedal. Ashley was distraught, and he didn't blame her. After learning about the confrontation she'd had with her mother, and adding Agatha's phone call to Uncle Graham, Phillip had no clue what kind of drama waited for them.

Before he knew it, they arrived, and he slowed in front of the beach house. An unfamiliar SUV was parked in the driveway.

"They never travel together." Ashley bit her lip as he killed the ignition. "And she's never without her staff."

Phillip shook his head. Agatha Cartwright couldn't get any worse. "Whatever happens, we roll with it. Deal?"

"Deal." Though she didn't sound convinced.

Phillip opened the door and went around to offer Ashley a hand. Together they strode up the front walk as Ashley death-gripped his hand.

She reached for her keys, but the door flung open. A visibly distraught Mary Beth stepped out and shut the door behind her.

Ashley moved to her best friend. "Are you okay, Mary Beth?"

"What do you think?" Mary Beth glanced over her shoulder at the closed door. "No offense, but your mother scares me."

"None taken. She scares me too." Both girls stood at the door for a long second before Ashley asked, "My dad is here?"

Mary Beth nodded solemnly. "Glenn is here."

"What are they doing?"

Mary Beth lifted her shoulders. "Your dad is reading the paper at our dining room table, and your mother is on the deck."

If Phillip hadn't known Agatha, he might have laughed because this sounded like a serious overreaction. But he knew better. "We can't stand outside all day. Let's go say hello."

Mary Beth groaned but stepped back, gesturing that he should go first. "Sure, of course. After you, brave soldier."

He rolled his eyes and shook his head, muttering, "It's not going to be that bad."

A mumbled "ha" trilled behind him, and Phillip didn't know if it came from Ashley or Mary Beth. They entered together and didn't hear a sound. It would've been normal, yet it was creepy. They walked closely together into a beach house that had become a house of horrors.

"Honey." The girls jumped at Ashley's father's voice as they rounded into the dining area.

Phillip rested his hand at the small of Ashley's back as her father continued. "We're sorry to drop in unannounced. Let me get your mother."

Her father offered her a stiff but friendly embrace then walked toward the sliding glass doors.

After both parents were on the deck, Mary Beth muttered, "Are we in the twilight zone?"

"Maybe," Ashley said. "But my dad has never been the problem. Guard your loins."

As if the *problem* needed an announcement, her dad walked in from the deck alongside Ashley's mother. The woman didn't look nearly as happy to be there as her husband, but Phillip couldn't exactly read her expression.

"Ashley Catherine." Her mother stopped midway across the living room, adding with small disdain, "And Phillip."

He nodded hello, taking his cue from Ashley, who didn't move to greet her mother.

"Why are you here?" Ashley demanded without any preamble.

"I thought I'd like to visit—" Agatha paused, most likely to rethink her explanation, as her husband gave her a quick nudge. "I wanted to follow up on our conversation."

Mary Beth gave Ashley a sorry-but-not-sorry look then excused herself from the room. Agatha eyed Phillip, silently encouraging him to do the same, but he didn't move a muscle.

"I suppose it's best you're here," her mother lamented.

"Would you like to have a seat?" Glenn headed toward his paper.

Still, Ashley didn't move. "Why didn't you call?"

Glenn folded the paper and glanced in between mother and daughter. "We had to talk on the drive here."

"You *drove* here this morning?" Ashley moved to the table and pulled out a seat.

Wow. Phillip calculated how long the drive would take. It was at least several hours.

"You didn't have to do that," Ashley said.

"We did after our heated discussion last night. It gave us a chance to speak with cooler heads." Glenn glanced at Agatha. "Sit down, Aggi."

Uncomfortably, Ashley's mother joined her husband at the table.

Her dad continued. "It occurred to us that we needed to have a face-to-face conversation." Glenn glanced at Phillip. "With you also. Please join us."

Again, after reading Ashley's unspoken cues, Phillip chose the seat next to her. Agatha pulled out the seat next to her husband, paused, then sat across from Ashley on the other side of her father.

Isn't this cozy…

"I said what I needed to say before," Ashley said.

"But we didn't," her dad said, letting his gaze linger on his wife.

Agatha cleared her throat. After she shifted and fidgeted, she looked her daughter in the eye. "I'd like to apologize. To both of you." The hard mask of the woman's expression cracked, and what might have been sorrow creased her forehead as she glanced between the two of them. "I've never been the best…"

"Mother," Ashley suggested.

The cold bitterness in her voice caught Phillip off guard.

But Agatha nodded. "Yes, *mother*. I tried, but not always and especially failed you when it counted."

Ashley's hand dropped under the table and found Phillip's. He grasped it, running his thumb over her knuckles as her fingers tightened. Ashley pulled in a deep breath, relaxing as she let it out. "Before you say anything else, Mother, I decided last night to let everything in the past go, to forgive everything between us."

Her admission rolled through him with a thunderous shock. He didn't know if he had that in him.

Ashley's fingers squeezed his again, and she awkwardly laughed. "It turns out that making decisions to magically change how I feel doesn't fix everything. But I think it might have helped."

"Ashley Catherine—"

"Mother, *my name is Ashley*."

Her mother's mouth snapped shut as though she'd been slapped, but then she tried, "Ashley."

"Thank you."

Her mother nodded. "I appreciate that you can imagine forgiving me. That kind of heart comes from your grandmother." She let her eyes roam the dining and living room. "Maybe that's why she made sure that you inherited this house—to fix my mistakes. Maybe she knew about you two."

Her thoughts seemed to linger until Glenn cleared his throat. Then Agatha took a deep breath. "Phillip, you came to us, trusting that we would do what would be best for Ashley Cath—*Ashley*. But I used that trust against you, and for that, I apologize."

Having heard the heartbreaking details from Ashley earlier, he didn't expect the knot that tied in his throat.

"I don't expect you to accept my apology," Agatha continued. "But I have something for you that I hope will start our journey of forgiveness."

Glenn took a manila envelope from under his newspaper and handed it to Agatha. She unfolded the top and pulled out a set of keys.

"This is yours, and we are more than happy to support your nonprofit," her mother said.

His keys. Ashley gasped. Phillip couldn't breathe.

"Glenn and I spoke about what happened, what was said, what I did…"

"And we'd like to correct the past," Glenn said. "Aggi and I both know how hard you've worked to help others. It makes you a responsible, thoughtful young man. Though you don't need to hear that from us to know it's true."

Her mother handed Phillip the keys. Holding them sent a shock of electricity through him. "But I can't."

Agatha gave an exaggerated chortle that leaned more friendly than sarcastic. "Well then, good luck finding a lawyer to undo that mess," she awkwardly joked. "Inside the envelope, you'll find the paperwork that has already been signed to you as a gift."

Phillip pulled the paperwork from the envelope. There was his name, and even as he stared at it, it didn't change. This wasn't a dream, and gratefully, he glanced from Ashley's mother to her father and back again. "I don't know what to say."

"Mother," Ashley whispered. "That's so—"

Agatha raised her hand. "Before you—rightfully, I suppose—question my motives, I'd like to be perfectly up-front. This is not an attempt to buy either of your forgiveness." Her voice cracked, and she took a moment to smooth the sleeve of her shirt. "But a donation to a wonderful cause and a meaningful gift to someone I wronged. One day, I would like all of us to be okay."

Under the table, Ashley and Phillip's grip tightened. He couldn't see into the future, but he already believed it would be better than okay. Somehow, he knew Ashley believed that too.

With that, the overwhelming conversation ended. Ashley invited her parents to stay, and Mary Beth came out from likely eavesdropping. They decided on an afternoon meal on the deck.

Ashley curled into Phillip's lap on the outdoor couch. He stroked her hair and listened as she quietly pointed out her parents' surprising behavior. Phillip was equally surprised but kept his comments to himself as Ashley marveled over her dad managing the gas grill.

But even he couldn't stop himself from whispering, "What's happening?" when Glenn convinced Mary Beth to help him chop vegetables as his sous chef, then when her mother butted in to show everyone how chopping vegetables should be done. Before their very eyes, Glenn demanded that *Aggi* loosen up and help him prep kabobs. Phillip expected a scene, but as soon as Agatha got her hands dirty, a switch flipped. The queen of perfection started to have fun.

Ashley turned to Phillip. "Oh my God, I can't believe I forgot to tell you. This afternoon has been so crazy."

"What?" he asked.

"Mary Beth is moving out!"

"What?"

Ashley shrugged. "It's a bit of a long story that I'll tell you later, but she was concerned that I was selling the house."

His eyebrows lifted. "This house?"

She laughed. "Like I said, a very long story, but the situation was concern enough to give her the nudge to take a job at a fancy accounting firm that she would never admit to herself she wanted. It's in DC."

"Wow."

"So…" She propped her chin on his shoulder. "After she finds a place to rent, I'll be here all alone in this big house."

Phillip eased back and studied her eyes. "As it turns out, I happen to have a place in DC that will be for rent soon."

"Really?" She grinned mischievously. "I didn't know."

"It's a bit new. I'm moving in with my girlfriend."

She beamed. "You are?"

"I am. Though I'm only calling her my girlfriend for now. One day soon, she'll be my wife."

The Next 7 Brides for 7 Blackthornes Book!
There's more Blackthorne excitement ahead. Don't miss
BROCK by Roxanne St. Claire!

ABOUT THE AUTHOR

Cristin Harber is a *New York Times* and *USA Today* bestselling romance author. She writes sexy romantic suspense, military romance, new adult, and contemporary romance. Readers voted her onto Amazon's Top Picks for Debut Romance Authors in 2013, and her debut Titan series was both a #1 romantic suspense and #1 military romance bestseller.

Join the newsletter! Text TITAN to 66866 to sign up for exclusive emails.

The Titan Series:
Book 1: Winters Heat
Book 1.5: Sweet Girl
Book 2: Garrison's Creed
Book 3: Westin's Chase
Book 4: Gambled and Chased
Book 5: Savage Secrets
Book 6: Hart Attack
Book 7: Sweet One
Book 8: Black Dawn
Book 9: Live Wire
Book 10: Bishop's Queen
Book 11: Locke and Key
Book 12: Jax
Book 13: Deja Vu

The Delta Series:
Book 1: Delta: Retribution
Book 2: Delta: Rescue*
Book 3: Delta: Revenge
Book 4: Delta: Redemption
Book 5: Delta: Ricochet
*The Delta Novella in Liliana Hart's MacKenzie Family Collection

The Only Series:
Book 1: Only for Him
Book 2: Only for Her
Book 3: Only for Us
Book 4: Only Forever

The ACES Series:
Book 1: The Savior
Book 2: The Protector
Book 3: The Survivor

7 Brides for 7 Soldiers:
Ryder (#1) – Barbara Freethy
Adam (#2) – Roxanne St. Claire
Zane (#3) – Christie Ridgway
Wyatt (#4) – Lynn Raye Harris
Jack (#5) – Julia London
Noah (#6) – Cristin Harber
Ford (#7) – Samantha Chase

7 Brides for 7 Blackthornes:
Devlin (#1) – Barbara Freethy
Jason (#2) – Julia London
Ross (#3) – Lynn Raye Harris
Phillip (#4) – Cristin Harber
Brock (#5) – Roxanne St. Claire
Logan (#6) – Samantha Chase
Trey (#7) – Christie Ridgway

Each Titan, Delta, Aces, and 7 Brides book can be read as a standalone (except for Sweet Girl), but readers will likely best enjoy the series in order. The Only series must be read in order.

Printed in Poland
by Amazon Fulfillment
Poland Sp. z o.o., Wrocław

50776738R00125